Dear Mark

Hope you enjoy the book

Zend ABN

ANGEL WINGS

PAW-PRINTS ON
THREE CONTINENTS

ABHI

PARTRIDGE

ISBN: Softcover   .   978-1-5437-6148-1
            eBook   978-1-5437-6149-8

To order additional copies of this book, contact
Toll Free +65 3165 7531 (Singapore)
Toll Free +60 3 3099 4412 (Malaysia)
orders.singapore@partridgepublishing.com

www.partridgepublishing.com/singapore

CONTENTS

"*The world was conquered through*
the understanding of dogs,
the world exists through the understanding of dogs."
Friedrich Nietzsche

PREFACE

This travelogue was born from a blog that we wrote on our coast-to-coast trip in the summer of 2017. *"Wouldn't it be fun if Zen were to write the blog?"* Zen was our two-year-old Lab. Thank you, Julia Randell-Khan, for the suggestion. Our followers loved Zen's funny and conversational tone. Gorgeous photos, taken by my beautiful wife, Anju, added spice to the narrative. This trip wouldn't have come to fruition without her endurance and tolerance. She does not like road trips, and she also had to put up with my quirks for two months. It was a giant leap of faith for her, and I owe her my utmost. The trip helped hone her iPhone photography technique. Behind every man, there is a successful woman.

The first draft of the book was completed in November 2018 during NaNoWriMo(National Novel Writing Month), an annual worldwide challenge to write 50,000 words.

I will be forever grateful to my brother, Ashish, who had been kind enough to read the first draft and give his thoughts on the story and the characters.

Charu, my spiritual anchor, introduced the joys of canine companionship to our family. Without her, there wouldn't be a story.

This book was made possible with the encouragement of Dr. Phil Pizzo and my Stanford DCI colleagues. My deep gratitude to the Djerassi group - Sydney Macy, Susan Nash, Mary Ittelson. Donna Slade, the indestructible and inspirational Richard Chow, Paula Pretlow, Jim Scopa, and Big Red Jim Weitrich, for reading part of the manuscript and offering me detailed suggestions. I am indebted to my barn mate - Melissa Dyrdahl- a fellow dog lover and beta reader, for her thoughts.

My fantastic editor, Therese Arkenberg, helped me transform a shaky 60,000-word story into a compelling read.

The illustrations are hand-drawn by Aditya Phadke, an extraordinarily talented artist. Thank you for making the story immersive. A big thank you hug to Samara Baidwan, a budding artist in middle school, for the cute transition image sketches.

This book wouldn't be worthy of reading without the special attention John Evans gave to parts of the manuscript. His detailed feedback - handwritten and electronic, was an essay by itself.

I will be forever beholden to Ram Kapoor, whom I bombarded with emails and Whatsapp messages, for pushing me along to complete it.

Finally to all the friends who hosted us at home to make this the most memorable trip of a lifetime:

Anand, Sadhana, Sanjana and Rohan in New Jersey,

Sydney and Tom in Colorado,

Tushara for allowing Zen to run wild in her mansion,

Indu and Ram - our journey began and ended in their home in Orinda.

CHAPTER 1

Do Dogs Go to Heaven?

The Righteous One was the eldest of the Five brothers. He never lied. He ascended to heaven when his time on earth came to an end. His dog accompanied him on the journey. They were both allowed to enter by the resident God.

Dr Boon came in, checked his vitals, and said, "Let me know when you are ready."

We will never be ready, but this is the best thing for him, I thought. *He is not leading a good life. He was supposed to have a long, happy life when we got home. This isn't long. Life is so unfair.*

Do dogs go to heaven? This thought coursed through my head as we sat with Zen in the vet's clinic in Singapore. It was a week before Thanksgiving. Today was the day. I had planned this day for a week without telling anyone. It was my cross to bear.

The room was small. We, his humans, crowded around our pup. He was sitting on his favorite blue rug, his useless hind legs sticking out in front like two sticks. An unnatural pose, which we had grown used to in the last six months. The mood was somber. Zen had the goofy look that we loved, the one that said "Life is always fun. What's with you guys?" There was a ragged edge to his breathing, but he never liked vet clinics. Not here, not even in California, where he spent the best years of his life. He did grab their treats, though.

My mind was replaying an Indian mythological story called the Mahabharata. It is about an epic clash between two dynasties. One led by the Righteous One and his four brothers. The other led by a blind king with a hundred legitimate sons and a few illegitimate ones. To add spice to the ancient soap opera, all the warring parties were cousins. Sharing the same DNA makes for better storylines. The Five brothers believed that their cousins had usurped their kingdom. This war was one of justice, to be the rightful ruler of the kingdom.

Why am I even thinking of this? Is this my way of dealing with the inevitability of the next few minutes? The vet had assured me that it will all be over in a minute and that he will feel no pain.

Our lives changed irrevocably four months after we left California to come home, to Singapore. It was a hot Saturday afternoon outside. We were going about our everyday lives inside. The air conditioner was humming.

Zen was scarfing down his dinner. I was half asleep on the couch and our (my and Zen's) significant other was reading. I heard Zen playing with our helper, and then a small yelp. I looked up and saw him sitting on the carpet, looking a bit shocked.

"What happened?" I asked our helper as I felt his leg to see if it was hurting.

"Don't know, sir. We were playing and he sat down."

I stood him up so I could feel his knees and his hips. He had suffered a knee injury a year ago and I feared a relapse. There was no reaction from him as I pressed what I thought was his injured knee. *Hmm. No pain there.* He tried to take a few steps and collapsed. A sense of dread began to overcome me. *Is it a spine injury?*

We stood him up again. He collapsed again. At that time, I knew. It was a spinal issue and not muscular. He was now in excruciating pain. He was breathing heavily and whimpering ever so lightly. He never whimpered. His feet were stretched out in front of him, muscles locked, like in rigor mortis. The vet later said that it is a natural reaction to an extreme injury.

The next few hours went by in a blur as we raced to the emergency vet, admitted him and shot him full of painkillers. An MRI revealed that he had a spinal embolism. His disc had ruptured and the fluid inside had shot out like a bullet and hit his spine. The damage was unknown. The consequence was known—paralysis of the hindquarters. He couldn't walk, he couldn't wag his tail, he couldn't pee. Strangely enough, he could poo. Only time would tell if he would recover from it.

The vet was optimistic. "Eighty percent of dogs recover from this injury," she said. "He will need a lot of therapy and physio. Try acupuncture, hydro, but please don't give him Chinese medicines."

Zen, like all animals, came to terms with his disability and had adapted. He would scoot around on his butt in a very endearing manner. It was funny. It was also his way of telling us, "I have dropped some poop in my wake. Please pick it up." Food still made him very excitable. Bright eyed, mouth open in a goofy grin, he would rotate around himself, using his hind legs like anchoring poles. He would look forward to his hydrotherapy because he got his favorite cheese and sausage treats.

How is he so happy? I would wonder and marvel. *I should learn positivity from him.*

For six months, we tried every possible treatment to give him the best chance of recovery. Modern and rational ones from Western medicine. Ancient ones developed by the Chinese and the Indians. Karmic and tantric treatment invoking the inner being and the sense of touch to transfer healing power from my body to his.

Nothing worked.

Our gods had ordained that his time with us must come to an end. A million Hindu gods, not one decided that he should recover. It was a true test of my faith or the lack of it.

"It's time." I threw the words out there in the small room, somehow wishing they were not true.

Zen looked at us, as if to ask, "What's up, guys? What's with all that facial water?" He had a keen sense for detecting grief or sorrow.

The vet came in and administered the sleeping meds. As they took effect, our pup lay down on his rug, the rug that he had slept on for the last two years, the familiar smell and the soft texture giving him comfort and security. He closed his eyes and gave his usual deep sigh, a signature expulsion of breath that indicated all was well in his world. It was his way of telling us, as he did every day, that he was going to sleep. He was going to play with his buddies in his dreams, yipping and yapping. He was going to his happy places—Bedwell Park and the Stanford trail.

I came out of the clinic and stood in the hot midmorning sun. Dr Boon came out, gave me a hug and said, "He had a very good life. I don't know of any dog that traveled so much and had so much fun. You guys loved him."

"Thank you," I mumbled.

A few days later, we visited his favorite place. We had one final ritual to complete. It was a winter morning. The air was crisp and the sun was slowly warming the meadow. The flock of geese were gathered in their habitual spot in the middle. We opened the urn and scattered his ashes. A gentle breeze came in from the sea and bore them heavenward. As I watched them dance lazily upwards, I thought of him charging at the flock of geese to get them airborne in a frenzy of honking before returning to my side with a goofy grin, saying, "Did you see that? It was awesome," then turning around and taking off to play with one of his buddies.

Yes. He is in his heaven.

PART 1

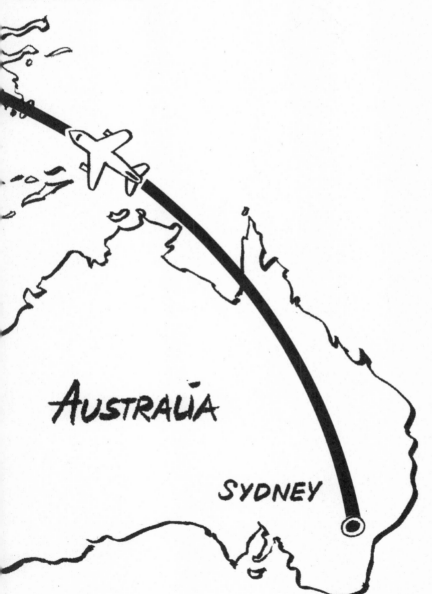

CHAPTER 2

"His Eyes Are Talking to Me"

"Here, doggy.... Come here, Zen," crooned DC in a futile attempt to entice me into a large box which looked like the one I had entered as a puppy. It could easily hold two of me and seemed to be airy. A mesh window on each side and a large main door for a comfortable entry completed the box. Humans called it a crate. A sense of foreboding enveloped me as I thought of the little crate that I had foolishly stepped into and the horrifying trip that I took to get here, the trials and tribulations. The noise, the abrupt movements, the smell, the sick feeling...

I sat down and gave DC a look. *No way, Jose—I ain't going in there!*

This moment arrived a couple of months after I had joined AC, DC, and Mon Ami in an apartment in sunny Singapore. It evoked some very unpleasant memories.

The first sensation I can recall is the cold as I emerged from my mother's warm womb. I could feel her licking me, cleaning me up, readying me for the world. I couldn't see a thing, but I could feel another body close to me and I snuggled in for warmth. *Ah! That's nice*, was my last thought before I fell asleep.

"Cassador Simba." I heard the words and felt a pair of warm arms holding me. I wriggled and shoved my nose closer to the sound. *Who is this creature and what is it saying?* I could make out a hazy shape through my unfocussed eyes. My vision was undeveloped; my nose wasn't. I navigated the world with my nose from the day I was born. The shape smelled interesting, different from my siblings and my mother. I strained closer for a sniff and was rewarded with a chin which tasted soft and creamy.

"Oh! My first kiss!" exclaimed the shape, giving me a long cuddle.

I heard another voice say, "Is that what you want to call him, Cathy?"

"Yes. It sounds very royal and he is a special pup."

I grew braver as the days went by, and exploring the wide-open green area outside the house became my favorite activity. I would shoot out the door whenever it was opened and stay out till Cathy came looking for me (It was very cold, so Cathy did not allow us to be out for very long. My mom obviously had adult privileges so she could stay out as long as she wanted, but we pups were

12

time restricted). A new experience waited on the other side of that door every day. One day, it was these loud clucking creatures that ran away when I exploded into the outside. I would chase them just for the fun of it. They always outran me and if I got too close, they ran in the air, much faster than they could on the ground. Another day, my wanderings brought me up against four trees. They smelled funny. As I was sniffing at one of them, something large came down and knocked me over. I yelped in surprise. As I scrambled to my feet, I heard Cathy say, "Simba, be careful. Those cows can be nasty." Those words would stay with me and pop into my head on another continent a few years later.

Official records at the Australian Kennel Club show my birthplace as Cassador Retrievers, Gatton, Queensland. I would discover this eighteen months later when two kids barged into my life and used the Internet to pull up my family history. They told me, "Zen, did you know your dad's name is Cassador Pride and your mom is a chocolate Lab? You got your brown eyes from her."

Life went by in a blur, as it always does when it is fun—an endless cycle of eat, sleep, play, and poop, in no particular order. One day, Cathy put this small box in front of me and threw in my favorite treat. "Here, Simba, get it!"

Food-motivated that I am, I quickly scrambled in, and as I was scarfing my treat, I heard the click of a door closing behind me. I turned around and saw a steel mesh between me and freedom. It bewildered me. I could see Cathy on the other side. Trying to get out, I bumped my nose into the mesh. I whimpered to Cathy, "Please let me out. What are you doing? Why have you put me in this box?"

This box was going to be my home for the next seventy-two hours.

"He is good to go. Bye, sweetheart, we will miss you," said Cathy. She put her fingers through the mesh, but I was too scared to lick them.

"Okay," I heard a strange voice say. Then my whole world moved—a strange sensation. I yelped in panic. There was a thump as I was placed in another, larger box and the door was shut. Another motion, more rhythmic, began, which I would discover later was a van driving.

I was twelve weeks old and I had no clue what was coming next. So, as we all do in the animal kingdom, I quietly resigned myself to my fate and waited it out. The next seventy-two hours were an endless onslaught of new smells, new sights, and new sounds: the quiet rumble of truck tires on the highway, some high-pitched screaming sounds which hurt my ears, the smell of sea air, and the powerful stench of something unknown.

"Good day, mate. Shipment to Singapore. Where should I leave it?" I heard the voice say to someone.

"Are his export documents in order?" another strange voice replied.

"Yes."

"Alright then, load it on that pallet and we will take it from here."

I was in a large room till the sun went down and it became dark outside. I heard a whining sound, and my box was moving in the air, like those clucking creatures back at the farm. The mouth of a tunnel came into my limited view and I was swallowed by the darkness. There were a few clicks and then it went quiet. I couldn't smell any humans. All the other smells were unfamiliar. A quiet hum vibrated through the darkness and we moved again, this time more gently. After a few minutes, the vibrations increased and the hum crescendoed to a shriek. My head hurt and I cowered in fear. *What was that sound?* For what seemed like a very long time, I couldn't stand in my box. Whenever I tried, I kept falling against the side. I curled myself into a ball, whimpering in panic. Cathy was not there to pick me up and calm me down.

After a few minutes, the shriek had subsided to a low, urgent hum. I slowly regained my feet, took a step to the front of my cramped accommodation, and sniffed. Nothing familiar. The tunnel was not so dark anymore and I could see other boxes. No sound came from them. There was no sign of life. I lay down, exhausted, and promptly fell asleep.

An urgent need to pee woke me up and I instinctively walked toward the door, but nobody opened it for me. I desperately tried to hold it, but failed. The smell of my own pee overwhelmed me. I tried to move away from it.

I couldn't. The towels laid out at the bottom of my box were now soaked. I found a dry spot and sat down, trying to lick myself clean. *God! This is disgusting!*

A sudden thump and a violent shaking woke me up from my slumber. *What was that?* I was again thrown around in the box. My right paw hurt. The shaking went on for an eternity. My heart raced. Panic was setting in. *Where is Cathy? Where is my mom? Someone, please help. Please!*

The shaking subsided. An awful smell clung to me like a blanket. *God! What is it?* I looked around, searching, sniffing for the source. It was me! The violent shaking had splashed me with my intestinal deposits. Gross! *Never again,* I promised myself. *Never again will I ever get into another box in my life again!*

The hum slowed down and an unknown sensation washed over me. My ears started hurting again, I felt queasy; I just wanted to lie down and die. There was a bump, the hum rose again, and the tunnel slowed to a stop. A door opened and I could smell fresh air, fresh moisture-laden air. A human came toward my box. There were a few clicks, my box started moving, and I emerged from the tunnel. It was very hot. The sun's rays were blinding. After a short ride, my box was deposited in a room, out of the sun and away from the heat. I could hear footsteps.

"Alamak! You stink," said an unfamiliar voice. The tone indicated "female." Peering through my mesh, I could make out the shape of a person, at least two heads shorter than Cathy.

Sure, lady, you also would if you had no place to go for twenty-four hours!

I heard her call out, "Oi...come here and give this guy a bath!" Or at least that's what I thought she said. Her words sounded very different from Cathy's and I hadn't quite understood what they meant.

A man opened the mesh door and grabbed me. His touch was hard, not as tender as Cathy's. His hands did not smell like her's. In twelve weeks, I could make out the difference between a man and a woman. The frequency of a man's voice is lower than a woman's. Men also smell different. He put me in a tub and turned on the water spray. The shock of the cold water evoked a yelp and I tried jumping out of the tub. He grabbed me tightly and I yelped again.

"Oi...what you doing? Go easy. That's an expensive puppy. Don't kill it la!" said the female voice.

"Sorry, Jackie. He dirty. Have to spray a bit harder. Have pee and poo all over him."

If Cathy were to look at Jackie, she would see a slim Chinese woman with short black hair and an intense manner about her. She was the owner of a pet shop in central Singapore, which was to be my new home for the foreseeable future. The store was not very big. It had two levels. The upper level was Jackie's warehouse, and all the residents—we puppies—lived on the ground floor.

The "Puppy Residences" were cages stacked one on top of the other, three high. All the cages were of the same size, which was not a problem for the little guys. It was cramped for us big guys. I could just about stand and move a foot in either direction. The lower level held all the "big dogs," with me being one of them. The upper cages were for the little ones. A metal tray covered with newspapers was laid out on the floor of the upper cages to stop the little ones peeing and pooping on the big ones. We were let out of our cages twice a day, into a small room, to eat and do our business. No playtime! Our only human contacts were Jackie and the Man. He always smelled of pee and he never said a word unless it was to yell at us. We were all quite scared of him and tolerated him only because he kept our cages clean. In my head he was Loud Man. Eat, sleep, poop, no play...that's what my life had become. I thought of how everything had changed in seventy-two hours. From the freedom of a farm to caged captivity in a small room. A sense of despair hung over the Puppy Residences.

The biggest deception of World War II

Singapore had been a British colony since 1819. The British had a large contingent of troops stationed there during WWII. It was a strategic prize for the invading Japanese army. On the night of Feb 8th, 1942, the Japanese attacked Singapore. General Yamashita, famously known as the Tiger of Malaya, wanted a quick victory. The Commonwealth forces, led by General Percival, outnumbered the Japanese invasion forces by 3:1. Fully aware of the numerical superiority, Winston Churchill had famously ordered General Percival, "The battle must be fought to the bitter end at all costs... Commanders and senior officers should die with their troops. The honor of the British Empire and the British Army is at stake." Yamashita attacked ferociously and, through a mixture of braggadocio and arrogance, managed to convince Percival that unconditional surrender was his only option. Believing that the ruthless Yamashita would massacre his troops and the citizens of Singapore, Percival opted to surrender. Little did he know that the Japanese were running low on ammunition, they had only one hour's worth of artillery shells, and their supply line was stretched to breaking point. If Percival had counterattacked then, it might have changed the course of history.

One day, I heard some voices in the outer room. Jackie was saying, "We have a Lab pup. He is about four months old and he is a purebred Australian."

"Okay. Can we see him?" a male voice replied.

"Sure. Oi...can you bring Rollo out?" Jackie had named me Rollo. Cassador Simba to Rollo was a downer, but I liked Jackie. She reminded me of Cathy.

Loud Man opened my cage and escorted me into the anteroom. Three heads were looking at me through the glass window that separated the anteroom from the main shop. A man head and two women heads. One was bigger than the other.

"Aww…. He's so cute," said the little woman's head.

The other one nodded and said, "Toye." By now I had come to understand this term, which meant "Yes" or "Okay" as the situation demanded.

Big Head, the man, asked, "Can we go inside and see him?"

"Sure," said Jackie.

Big Head and Little Head came in and I promptly jumped on Little Head with pure, unadulterated joy, wagging my tail furiously, my hips doing all sorts of gyrations.

"NO!" I heard Jackie yell.. I ignored her and focused on Little Head. I really needed to be super cute and get the hell out of the Puppy Residences.

"Awwwww. He is so cute! Can we get him, Papa?"

Big Head, or Papa, turned to Jackie and asked: "How much for him?"

"Seven thousand dollars. But I can come down to six thousand five hundred if you buy NOW."

"Wah lao…why so expensive?"

"He has pedigree papers la!"

"No need…too much money for a dog. Let's go…. We see another shop," Big Head told Little Head. With that, they walked out, and so did my exit pass from the Puppy Residences.

Humans came and went and I was still in this cage. The bars of the cage increasingly pressed closer. I was growing and soon the cage became too small for me. I could just about turn around. Every time I stood up, my head hit the roof. *Why don't people like me? Am I too big? Am I too playful? Am I too expensive?* These thoughts kept circling in my head. If dogs could get depressed, I was clearly headed toward becoming a basket case.

Big humans and little humans came and looked at me, but I stayed in my cage. Over time, my mind accepted the cage as my sanctuary, a steel-reinforced protected area that gave me a feeling of security, even though all was not well in my world. Maybe my primitive wolf brain regarded it as my den. I could retreat to the farthest corners and sleep. *Yes, sleep is the panacea for all problems in my world. Feel sick…sleep. Feel depressed…sleep. Feel relaxed…sleep.* And so the days went by. I rarely saw any sunshine or rain. The room we were in had no windows, and we could only feel the tropical heat radiating from the walls or hear the steady thrum of rain accompanied by loud claps of very noisy BOOMS. Thankfully, it was cool inside. There was a box above our heads which blew cold air all the time.

On a particularly rainy and boomy day, I again heard some voices.

"Can we take a look at the Lab and the golden?" a voice was saying in a different tone from the ones that I had heard so far. It sounded very Indian. I had learned to understand the different sounds and tones—Chinese was more sing-song, Indian was flat, Australian like Cathy's was languid with much tongue rolling.

"Yeah. You call me this morning, right?" said Jackie.

"Yes, I did."

"Oi, can you bring out Mia first, then Rollo?"

Loud Man came around and let Mia out of her cage and into the anteroom. Indian Accent came into the room and cast an expert eye over a cowering Mia. Mia had been a return guest in the Puppy Residences. A couple had taken her a month ago but brought her back, saying she was too nervous and not a friendly dog. Blah! You spend seven months in a cage and you will also become a neurotic wreck.

Mia was put back in her cage and I was trotted out. The show animal in the bidding auction ring. I promptly peed on the linoleum floor. So much for pedigree—I was behaving like the village mongrel. Loud Man cursed under his breath and put me back in the cage while he cleaned up the mess.

I noticed this tall figure looking at me through the glass window separating the human world from my prison. I could make out only the head, oval-shaped, framed by dark, short hair. The eyes held an intense curiosity flecked with hints of sadness. I stared back unblinkingly. We were having an unspoken conversation through the glass, across ten feet of tiled space. The head turned to Indian Accent and said "Him," pointing at me. "Let's take him home. His eyes are talking to me."

With those words began my journey into their world. A world with no cages, though they did buy me one for reasons I will describe later; a world with good food, constant companionship, and complete freedom. A world where I could run unhindered across open fields, chase butterflies, and splash in puddles. A world where I could meet other dogs, cats, fish, humans, and any other creature living in the neighborhood.

My transition to this utopian world wasn't as easy as it sounds. As a species, we deal badly with sudden change. In the space of an hour, I was taken from the little room and even smaller cage to a huge room and no cage. My first steps outside the shop into the warm evening sunlight were terrifying. I had never stepped outside the shop. All my senses were in a frenzy. New smells, new sounds, new sniffing areas, and new people. The tsunami of stimuli overwhelmed my senses, causing panic in my puppy brain. Indian Accent took me to a car, picked me up, and put me in the back. The car was foreign to me; its movement wasn't.. After a while we reached a tall building, parked, and entered a small box that moved up and down. Over time, I would recognize the word "elevator." I entered my new world through a door which opened into a large room. The floor was slippery. There were big pieces of cloth and wool lying around. A big open space with metal bars, like my cage, overlooked a wonderful landscape of houses and trees. I could see people and their dogs walking on the street below. Later I would learn that it was called a balcony.

My new world had three companions: AC (Amenable Companion), DC (Disciplinary Companion), and Mon Ami - "My Friend" in French, for those of you who don't speak that fine language. The French bulldog residing above me in the Puppy Residences taught me a few important words and phrases, some of them very colorful. AC was the oval-shaped head with dark hair and captivating eyes, the one who had said, "His eyes are talking to me." I had already established a special connection with AC. I was able to get my way with the amenable persona. AC could always figure out my thoughts. Very uncanny. AC became my soulmate. DC was the one who brought me home. Firm but gentle and a creature of habit. Meals were always at a fixed time. Worked for me. I was never going to miss a meal with DC on overwatch. Walk timings and routes were pre-established. There was never a meandering walk with DC. DC was my teacher, dispensing the tough love that shaped me into a model canine citizen. DC reminded me of my mother, tolerant to a degree of nonsensical puppy behavior, but setting limits. I can still feel her gentle bite on my nose, a reprimand when I enthusiastically chewed her tail. AC was the rule breaker. Walks would be anytime. If the rule said, "dogs not allowed in here," AC would attempt to sneak me in. Over the next few years, I would attend classes in Stanford, get into a museum, and go shopping in Stanford mall, all accompanied by AC. I'd go places where a dog has never gone before. Mon Ami was the housekeeper. She kept the three of us well fed and well dressed. She was my constant companion who fed me, walked me in the evening, bathed me, and protected me from other dogs in the neighborhood. I didn't need the protection. I was a friendly soul, always wanting to play with the other brother or sister.

Night fell on that first day and the family was getting ready for bed. I wandered about the house, a restless soul, still unsure of where I would sleep. Where was my cage? My sanctuary. My den. I wished I could tell them, "You don't have my bedroom, my safe place from all the bad things in this world." So I moved about aimlessly, sat next to the bed, got up, walked around the house, sat next to the sofa. I was generally restless, stressed out and breathing heavily.

I heard AC asking DC, "Do you think he needs a crate?"

"He's a dog. He should be able to sleep wherever," said DC.

"I don't think so. I think he is missing his cage. He must be used to the one at the shop. Which pet shop is open at this time of the night? Maybe Pet Safari at Vivo City is open. Let me go and get him something."

I don't know how AC figured it out. *Finally! Someone gets it! Three cheers for AC. Hip hip hooray! Hip hip…*

An hour later AC came back with a portable wire enclosure. It was larger than the one in the shop. They set it up in their bedroom with a doggy bed as the base. I promptly entered it and settled down. The familiar smell and feel of the metal bars—aah! My sanctuary.

"See, I told you," said AC to DC. "He was missing his cage."

Tired from my exertions, I fell into a deep sleep.

My new world almost came to an abrupt end the next day. DC took me to the vet for my checkup. Town Vets is a small clinic on the ground floor of a tall block of apartments. The waiting area smelled of food, pee, and fear. I did not like going to such places. I could hear soft meowing sounds coming from behind a closed door. One door opened and a tall lady stepped out.

"Hi. Come on in," she said, greeting DC with a big smile. She had an easy, friendly manner and her voice sounded like Jackie with a bit of Cathy thrown in. She was also very thorough. She had me up on the examination table in a jiffy, all the time making cooing sounds which were meant to reassure me. Being on a steel table, five feet off the ground, is not reassuring. I froze like a statue. Of course, that helped her with the poking and prodding.

"Let's take a look here. What's his name?"

"Zen," said DC and got a puzzled look from her.

"Zen is now part of our lexicon at home. Everything is Zen doggy this and Zen doggy that. We figured it is more difficult to retrain us than to get him used to the name. So Zen it is. I told Clara at the reception to register him as Zen Jr."

"That's nice," she said.

All the while, she was checking my ears and running her hands down my flanks and legs. She put a cold, round object under my right armpit to listen to my heart.

"Okay. Heart sounds good, a bit fast, but he is a bit stressed, so no worries; spinal column shows no defect. Bone structure seems okay. See how his rear leg is splayed? It may be an indication of a potential hip problem. Also, his elbows are pronated, maybe something there later." DC was listening intently.

"Let's take a look at his teeth." She pried open my lips. "Okay, no puppy teeth. How old did you say he was?"

"Seven months," DC responded.

"Yeah. See, his front teeth are not aligned. His canines and molars seem okay. His right eye looks a bit infected. He has such gorgeous eyes." The last bit came out adoringly.

Then she ran her hands along my chest and stomach and... *Woah! Hey, lady, don't touch me there!* Her gloved hands were cradling my family jewels. Or my *only* jewel.

"He has an undescended testicle. Let me see if I can feel it in the canal." She pressed hard into my stomach and drew a glare from me.

"Can't seem to feel it. Maybe it is not formed.

"Good boy! You are such a sweetheart." I promptly unfroze and gave her my trademark tail wag. DC lifted me off the table and set me down on the floor.

"Here's the summary: he seems in pretty good condition other than his hips and the undescended testicle. We won't know the status of the hips till he is fully grown and we have him X-rayed. The undescended testicle will require surgery and since I can't feel it, we have to go in and take a look. Might be a mass of undeveloped tissue. You have to take it out, or else it may become cancerous. So, all in all, you may want to return him." Her tone was different. Not warm and cooing.

DC looked worried and I could feel the tension. "Take him back? Is it that bad?"

"It's your choice," she said.

My heart sank like a stone when I heard those words.

Take me back! Back to my prison! Back to Loud Man and the small room with no sunlight! Back to peeing on a newspaper!

Just when I thought my life had taken a turn for the better, I might be going back! My legs felt all wobbly. I sank to the cold marble floor. It smelled of antiseptic floor cleaner. The next few moments stretched into an eternity.

"I don't think we will do that," said DC. "He has been in that cage for four months and it would be cruel

28

to send him back. We will deal with the problems as they come up."

With those words, DC and AC won my undying loyalty. I would give my life for them! The floor was not so cold anymore. I was bouncing up and down, a goofy grin on my face, hips wiggling, tail wagging. *Yay!*

"Looks like he heard you!" said Dr. Boon. "Smart dog. I will prescribe some eye drops for the infection. Other than that, you are good to go."

I am not going back! Yipeeee dipeeee dooooo!

The apartment had a familiar, lingering aroma of another dog, not long gone. He was also called Zen. *Aha, that explains the talk with Dr Boon*, I thought. He was AC and DC's first dog and was solely responsible for AC's transformation from "I am terrified of dogs" to "His eyes are talking to me." AC had succumbed to Zen Sr.'s charms within a couple of months after his arrival into their house. His passing had left a massive void at home. AC and DC were bereft. Mon Ami would not have anybody to talk to the whole day. The apartment had become a sad place. My arrival, albeit a bit chaotic, made it into a happier one. The balcony became my fave place—"The World's Best Balcony," as DC would often refer to it fondly. I could see and smell the world go by. I also had a Zoomie room, the label I gave to the large living room. I would run like a maniac in there. DC referred to it as the Zen Zoomies. A Zoomie could be triggered at random. I would start running around—sometimes in circles, at other times in a straight line, wall to wall. Carpets and small pieces of furniture would get thrown around. I would begin at one end of the living room and run at full tilt across it into the waiting sofa for a soft landing among the cushions. Up and down a dozen times, and then I was spent, collapsing on the floor, chest heaving, and breathing labored.

As I grew more comfortable with the surroundings, my curious nature and the resultant wanderings that had got me in trouble at the farm came to the fore. My fear of the unknown, nurtured in the little room at the shop, dropped away. On a visit to a friend's house, I had explored their two-story apartment even before AC and DC finished walking in!

I had a problem, though. Two, in fact: loneliness and boredom. I had never stayed alone since the day I was born. I was with my mom and siblings at the farm. Later, I had the company of the tenants in the Puppy Residences. We discovered this problem only on my first weekend home alone. I will let DC tell you this story. It's called "I can eat your words."

It was the first Sunday after Zen's arrival into our household. Mon Ami was gone for the day, visiting her friends and her pastor. AC and I decided to step out for lunch. I wasn't sure how Zen would handle being alone for a couple of hours. Zen Sr. would just sleep behind the door till we came back. Of course, he was much older when he started doing that. In his younger days, we heard whines, yelps, moans, and other noises when we left him alone at home.

We snuck out when Zen was on the balcony, sleepily looking out and seeming to be on his way to snoozeland. A Nest camera was trained on the living room, to catch any action that happened in our absence. Twenty minutes later, we reached our favorite restaurant and ordered our usuals from the menu. While we were waiting for our food to be served, AC accessed the live feed. We couldn't see Zen, but we could hear a weird crackling sound in the background, like the one when the radio station is out of tune or when the signal is weak. We didn't think much of it and assumed it was the router or camera misbehaving. An hour later, on the way back home, we again accessed the live feed and heard the same crackling sound.

I must go and check out the mike, *I thought.* Maybe the plug is loose and causing the crackling.

We reached home, opened the door, and one wriggly, bouncy pup greeted us. The living room was a disaster zone. Shreds of the Straits Times, *the local newspaper, were strewn all over the floor. AC's 200-page banking report, a nice spiral-bound copy, lay in bits and pieces all over the carpet. We couldn't see much of the cover or the blue spiral binding.* Shoot, I hope he hasn't eaten it, *I thought. A frantic search yielded small pieces of the binding and one large piece of the glossy cover page. One eager beaver doggy was dancing around us, showing zero remorse at the destruction he had wrought. There was no guilty "I'm sorry" look. He seemed to be saying, "Don't you leave me*

alone again!" Having swallowed the newsprint and probably
a lot of plastic, he did not seem to be any worse for the wear
either. A wave of relief washed over me.

AC quipped, "Now I can tell my boss that my dog ate my
homework!"

Over the next few days, his output was speckled with bits
of blue and glossy plastic.

As the months passed, my extreme friendliness to
my species bloomed. I love dogs way more than humans.
I made new friends in Bea, a Singapore special—that's
what they lovingly call the local dogs—Ziggy, a feisty
Labradoodle, and Gryphon, a tough-as-nails older
Labrador. I was still working on being nice to human
strangers. Unannounced pats on the head and unasked-
for cuddles were not welcome and often resulted in low
growls and retreats (by me and not by the humans).
Strangely, the humans found it endearing. Funny
species. With them, nothing is ever at face value.
WYSIWYG (What You See Is What You Get) is not
in their dictionary. Unlike me, the master of non-verbal
communication, an open book for those who can read the
signals my tail, eyes, ears, mouth, and posture transmit.

One day, a large crate was brought in. Curious me
walked in tentatively, sniffed around, and did not like
it. It reminded me of the little crate that had brought
me into Singapore many months ago. A sense of dread
filled my being. Over the next few days, all my meals
were served inside the crate. I couldn't understand why.

However, food trumped any fears. I would walk in, wolf down my meal, and walk out.

A couple of weeks later, there was a lot of unusual activity in the house. Strange people walked in and started putting all our stuff into boxes. My favorite carpet and my even more favorite sofa got wrapped in paper and plastic. Packages disappeared out the front door and never came back. My routine was disturbed and I could sense that something was different. As evening fell, silence descended on our home and it was empty except for my food bowl, my toys, and a couple of chairs for AC and DC. Mon Ami came out of her room carrying her bag and I sensed she was sad. I could smell the salt water that flowed down her face. I had learned that when humans are sad or in pain, salt water comes out of their eyes.

In a broken voice, she said, "Goodbye, Zen. I go now and maybe I see you later." She bent down, patted my head, and gave me a tentative hug. I don't like hugs and usually tend to step away from one. This time I did not move and I gave her hand a reassuring lick. *Why is she sad? Where is she going? Why isn't she taking me for my evening walk?* She stood up, picked up her bag, and went out the front door. She never came back.

The next morning, a different man and woman walked in. I could smell other dogs on them. They were both very friendly. I heard him tell DC, "Let's puts him in the crate. We will take him to our office first, so he can settle down. Then we will put him on the flight tonight. Don't worry. I will send you pictures from Frankfurt. He should get into San Francisco around the same time as you."

DC turned to me and said, "Here, doggy. Come here, Zen." I balked. Then he tossed my favorite treat into the crate. Throwing caution to the winds, I chased it in and I heard the door close behind me.

PART 2

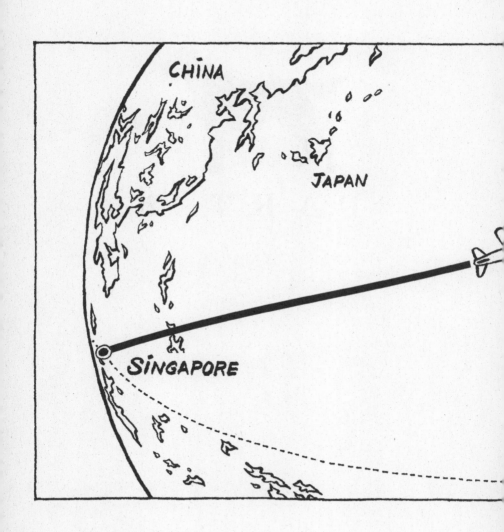

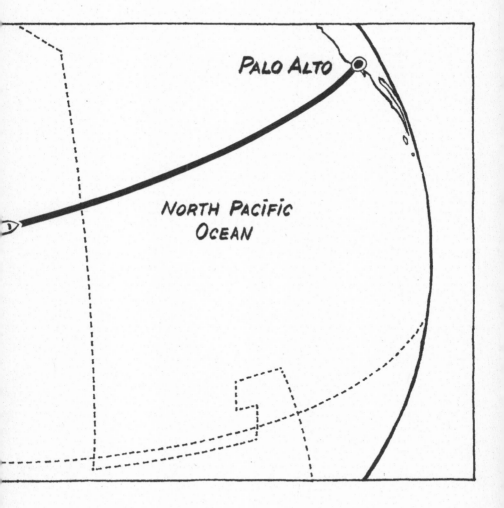

CHAPTER 3

Rites of Passage

I was back in a crate, strapped to a pallet and bumping my way to another plane. Yes, that's what they called those dark tunnels that make a ton of noise and give you a headache. This box was much bigger, with large openings on the side and in the front. All the openings were covered with a steel mesh. I could stand and move around. Rather plush.

Four months after I joined AC and DC, they decided to pack their bags and move 10,000 miles to another continent, North America. They had signed up for a fellowship at Stanford University, so we were headed to Palo Alto, California.

Palo Alto is named after a redwood tree which now stands at the intersection of Alma and El Camino Real. In 1776, Don Gasper de Portola, a Spanish explorer, was in the area with his team. Exhausted, they took a break under this tall redwood tree which resembled a tall stick. So, he named it El Palo Alto (Tall Stick). It is also the home of Stanford University.

Stanford is one of the largest universities in the world in land area.

The Cantor Museum has the largest collection of Rodin sculptures outside of Paris. Twenty major works are on display near the museum and on campus.
The museum also displays a series of stop-action photographs taken in 1877 showing, for the first time in history, that all four legs of a galloping horse can be off the ground.

There are two versions of how Stanford University began.

The fictional version: In the late nineteenth century, a man dressed in an old suit and a lady in a gingham dress presented themselves to the President at Harvard. They were Mr. and Mrs. Stanford. They told the president about their son, who had attended Harvard and recently died in an accident, and that they wanted to build a memorial in his name by funding a building. The president tried to dissuade them by saying that a building in Harvard would be expensive, implying that the couple, who did not look well-to-do, would not be able to afford it. The lady asked him how much money would be needed for the building. The president told her it would cost ten million dollars.

Hearing this, the lady turned to her husband and said: "Honey, if that's all it costs, why don't we set up a university on the West Coast?" And Stanford University was born.

The Real Life version: Leland Stanford was a multi-millionaire railroad magnate and the governor of California. He was the owner of Palo Alto Stock Farm, one of the premier ranches for breeding and training trotting horses on the West Coast. His only son, Leland Stanford Jr., died at the age of sixteen due to typhoid. The Stanfords set up the university as a memorial to him in 1891. They deeded a large fortune that included 8,000 acres, which subsequently became the campus.

I love the first version; it is more melodramatic.

Our new home was very different from the apartment in Singapore. It was a house with a garden. The main door and kitchen looked out onto the street in front and the bedroom windows faced the cross street. The walls were paper thin, letting the cold and the heat pass right through. Different sounds also made their way in, making for a very uncomfortable first few nights for all of us. I would growl and bark at the smallest crackle or snap. My humans were sleep deprived and unhappy. The house had a garden on one side bordered by a fence. DC's brother and his family lived in the house on the other side of the fence. They were looking forward to our arrival and welcomed us warmly. DC's nephews, Ash and Vini, had arranged a welcome gift for me as well: they had removed two boards from the fence to provide me easy access to their house. We used this gap to visit each other at all times. Ash was the dog lover, very talkative, with twinkling eyes and a ready smile. He taught me a few tricks, like begging on two legs for food. Why is that a trick? I will beg for food anytime, anywhere, and from anyone. Vini was the creative one, with an impish face and a permanent mischievous look. He lived in an imaginary futuristic, superhero-inhabited world. Star Wars was his favorite and he always wondered why there were no dogs in it. Maybe Luke Skywalker should have had one with laser eyes and other superpowers. They were my breakfast dates every day. These dates were to be life-altering for them a few months later.

I fell in love with the weather—so cool after the stifling heat of Singapore. The garden was my favorite place. I would chase squirrels, dig up the lawn, and bask in the sunshine. The garden also hosted my Zen Zoomies. It was much bigger than the Zoomie room in Singapore. I was so happy. There was always something interesting in every nook and cranny, especially in the spice garden. AC always knew where I had been when I came into the house smelling of some spice plant that I had trampled. I made a lot of new friends, both human and doggy, in the first few days. Almost everyone we met during a walk would want to say hi. I would respond in a frenzy of wiggling hips and swishing tail, eliciting cries of "Oh, he is so adorable," or "Soooo cute!" By now, I was more tolerant of the pat on the head and the unexpected cuddles. Meeting lots of friendly humans does that. I also intuitively sensed that the humans here loved dogs, a feeling I never got in Singapore.

My morning routine was: wake up...go for a walk... inhale all the lovely smells...romp in the garden...trot through the gap in the fence for breakfast with Ash and Vini before they went to school—they ate a tastier breakfast than AC and DC—and come back home to snooze. It was a dog's life!

Exploring my new neighborhood was a necessity. So many humans to meet, dogs to play with, and bushes to mark with my presence. Well...I sometimes forgot to mention to AC or DC that I was out exploring.

On one occasion, I walked out through the open front door and took a stroll around the block. AC and DC had never lived in a house before. DC would often forget to close the front door or would leave the garage door open and get an earful from AC.

"Hi, puppy. Are you lost?" I looked up from the interesting flowerbed that I was sniffing and saw a lady looking down at me. She reminded me of Jackie at the pet store in Singapore.

Am I lost? What is lost? Dogs don't get lost! We have a God-given navigational instinct which will lead us back home. If only there weren't so many distractions on the way....

While I was contemplating my reply, she came close to me and grabbed my collar.

"Where are your mom and dad?"

Back in Australia, but AC and DC are at home, I thought. *They are not my mom and dad; they are my companions.*

"Hmm...no contact details on your collar. Maybe you live around the corner." She tugged my collar and led me around the corner and lo and behold, there was AC, looking very anxious.

"Zen! Where did you go, puppy?" said AC in a worried tone.

"Is he yours?" said the lady.

"Yes," AC answered.

"I found him around the corner."

"Thank you so much. He must have wandered off through the garage while we were moving the furniture."

That wander resulted in a collar tag with my name and DC's mobile number. It came in very handy the next time I went for a walkabout and was found by a gentle old lady walking her dog. I went to say hi to the little guy and again got asked, "Hey, doggy, are you lost?" I ignored her. I was more interested in playing with the little guy. The old lady managed to collar me and call DC, who promptly trotted over and took me home after some profuse apologies and many ardent thank-yous. This escapade resulted in a baby gate being installed at the front door.

The excitement of a new country, new companions, and a new home also brought with it a loneliness in the new way of life. AC and DC would leave for Stanford and I would be alone at home with my thoughts for company and bored out of my doggy head. There was no Mon Ami chattering away in the kitchen and no balcony to look at the world go by. Dogs do funny things when they are left alone. Some bark incessantly at imaginary things, others pee and poo all over the house. I relieved my boredom by eating objects. Remember, I shredded AC's work report in Singapore.

This time, I chewed up DC's TV remote. My humans realized that in this new way of life, I would be alone quite a bit and therefore I needed to learn to be alone. DC figured out a way to fool my brain into being happy when they left me alone. For an extrovert dog like me, that should have been a challenge. It wasn't. I would get a treat to reward me for being alone. *Duh!* How does that work? I would be told, "Zen not coming" followed by a juicy bone. I would grab the bone and retire to the sofa. AC and DC would then leave the house while I was happily chewing away. From then onward, I would look forward to AC and/or DC leaving me alone and pointedly stare at the pantry door, behind which lay my treat bones. "Just give me one and get out of here," was my unbarked thought.

Another happy place was the Zen Cocoon—my plush crate that I had traveled in to Palo Alto. I had grown to love it and felt completely secure and comfortable in it. An orthopedic doggy bed just appeared when AC realized it was my happy place. I would sleep like a puppy, on my back with my feet splayed in midair, yipping and yapping while dreaming of all the fun I was having playing with my buddies. We were to move three times over the next two years. My Zen Cocoon was always in its rightful place, next to AC and DC's bed.

The steady hum of the tires on asphalt lulled me to sleep as we made our way toward San Francisco. It was a hot, sunny day and the van's air cooling box struggled to keep the interior cool. We were heading to Crossroads Cafe to meet AC and DC's college buddies, Rod and Isa.

Crossroads is an artsy cafe with a garden courtyard facing San Francisco Bay. It is one of the best dog-friendly cafes in town. The courtyard smelled of cheese and bread and dog. Rod and Isa were seated at one of the tables waiting for us. They were a contrasting couple. Rod was a huge guy with long hair, a soft voice, and a lot of hair around his mouth. He talked in hushed tones that belied his size and ability to do some serious damage if upset. Isa was petite, with a voice far bigger than her size. She was not a dog person and kept her distance from me.

"Hi, Zen," Rod said as he bent down to pat my head. His touch was soft. He got the obligatory hip wiggle and tail wag greeting.

Isa chose to ignore me and started talking to AC. "How are you? When did you get here? All settled in? How is the house?" The questions rolled off her tongue in rapid-fire fashion.

"Woah! Easy there, girl," said Rod. "Let's order some food and we can talk."

I was handsomely turned out in a new harness and a leather leash. DC tied me to a lamp post in the garden and they all sat down at a table nearby. I flopped down on the grass. The cool grass, the warm sun beating down on my back...I was headed to snoozeland!

"Hey big boy, want to play?" My ears perked up and my head turned toward the voice. A small dog was standing at the other end of the garden, inviting me to play: tail wagging, bouncing lightly on his front paws. "Come here. Let's play."

I shot off toward him. *Oh yeah!*

Bang! The leash brought me up short. *Dogza! I am tied up!*

I took off again. Bang! Again, I was brought up short and fell back. *Double Dogza! Once more to the fore*, said my brain and off I went a third time. This time I heard a loud "pop" and I was free and bounding toward him, scattering a few potted plants and trampling a few bushes on the way. I heard a lady scream in surprise. We took off, chasing each other around the garden, through the courtyard, toppling pots and ripping up flowers. There were more shouts and I heard DC say, "ZEN, STAY!"

There was only one word which could penetrate the happy fog in my brain when I was playing: "Stay." It meant I stopped wherever I was and stayed there. I stood in a ripped-up flower bed, panting happily and looking at my playmate bouncing around me.

DC walked over and grabbed my harness.

"Sorry about this. He just wanted to play with your dog. He is not aggressive. Just very playful with other dogs," he said to a shocked-looking lady, who had walked over to her dog.

"That's cool. He just surprised me," she said.

I was dragged back to the lamppost and tied up with the remainder of the leash, fully expecting a Bad Dog lecture.

"He busted a leather leash," DC said in an awestruck voice to Rod and the others. "Can you imagine? He broke his leash." There was an odd sense of pride in the voice. I did not get the lecture.

I rock! I broke my leash. Cool. Am I strong or what? That day at Crossroads will be etched in my memory forever: the day this big dog busted a leather leash!

California is a fun place for dogs. In fact, as I would realize later in the year, the whole country of the USA has a thing for dogs and they use every opportunity to express it. I can never walk down the street without a toddler or a pretty young thing (DC's words) coming across to say hi. I was SO the chick magnet (again DC's words).

Unlike Singapore, which has two seasons, hot and hotter, the US has many seasons: summer, autumn, winter and spring. Winter began soon after we arrived. Darkness fell earlier and it became colder. Our old house let all the cold in. Not that I minded. Nature had endowed me with a new winter coat. AC and DC weren't so fortunate. They had to go shopping for winter wear and room heaters. My exploratory streak caused them a lot of heartburn and anxiety on one of the shopping trips. This time I stepped out of DC's brother's home. AC, forever the one with the fear of losing me, has a vivid recollection.

DC and I had decided to go to Costco to pick up some winter jackets and look for a room heater. Zen was not at home. As usual he had gone for his breakfast date with Ash and Vini. I called my sister-in-law and she promised to keep an eye on him. We must have been gone for an hour when she called me. My blood ran cold when she said, "I can't find Zen."

"What do you mean, you can't find him?"

"He is not here and he is not at your place either. I checked." She was sounding very worried.

I hit the panic button. I told DC and we left our loaded cart in the aisle and ran out of the store. On the way home, images of him being run over by a car and lying bleeding in the street flashed into my head. "Maybe I shouldn't have asked her to look after Zen. She doesn't even like dogs." Where are we going to look for him? *the little voice in my head asked.*

We kept looking out of the windows as we drove home. Maybe we will see him sniffing in the bushes. Where is he? Oh God! I don't want to lose him like this, *said my little voice again.*

"Should we call 911?" I asked DC.

"Let's wait till we get home and look. Maybe he is back," DC, ever the optimist, replied.

Ash and Vini, having just come back from school, were waiting for us when we reached our house. So was their tearful mother.

I am so mad at her. *growled my little voice.*

We split up and went around the block calling his name, asking people on the street. Still no sign of Zen. No golden head peering through the bushes. I stood at the street corner, despondent, sure that my Zen was lost. The "Lost Dog" flyers

that I usually saw on our walks flipped through my head.
Now there would be one more.

"Hey…there he is. Zen! Zen," I heard Ash say from the
other side of the street. We looked and there was my puppy
running toward Ash.

I heard Ash calling me and I ran over to welcome
him. I loved Ash. AC came running over and gave me a
crushing hug. "Zen puppy…where did you go?"

Where did I go? I went for a wander, I thought to
myself.

I was going to wander a few more times over the next
year, worrying my humans. I always came back. They
didn't know that yet.

Halloween costume parties for dogs are a thing. Ash
and Vini decided that I was going to attend one in their
school. They dressed me up in my flaming neon orange
raincoat and took me to school as a firefighter. I got to
play with kids, and that was fun.

The evening, on the other hand, was unpleasant.
We went trick or treating on a street close to our home.
I was sniffing in a lawn and *click!;* something popped
up in front of my face and started talking to me in an
eerie voice. Shocked, I scrambled away, bowling over a
couple of kids. A few doors down, I got entangled in a
spiderweb woven of cotton and needed help to get free.
Ash and Vini picked up a lot of candy. I could not have
any of it—I'm not dieting, but chocolate is poisonous for
me and it can be fatal in large doses. Having said that, I

did see a big fat furry bro devouring a carelessly dropped slab of chocolate. He scarfed it down, packaging and all. There were bits of shiny silver foil hanging from his lips and he looked pleased as punch. Little did he know that a visit to the ER vet for a stomach pump was going to be the finale of his evening.

The new way of life was less kind to my companions. AC and DC had to do tons of housework: cooking, doing the dishes, laundry, cleaning, and vacuuming. There was no Mon Ami to help. I heard lots of arguments between them about doing these chores. I didn't have to do any— no opposable thumbs and all that. AC was a stickler for neatness and cleanliness. DC was not neat, and I unintentionally contributed to the mess. Most dogs shed hair. So did I, lots of it. DC was amazed how much hair I left on the sofa and on my bed.

AC decided that a good way to keep the house clean was to buy a round object. It would normally be sitting leashed to the wall. There was no smell and no reaction from it when I went close for a sniff. Nothing memorable about it, so I ignored it. One day I was alone, snoozing on the sofa. I heard a *click* and a *whirrr*. I sat up, looking for the source. The object had broken free of its leash and started wandering away. It was making a whirring sound and eating my hair off the floor. I thought only dogs ate food from the floor!

As the dog in charge of the house, I jumped off and approached it, thinking that I could stop it. It didn't stop. It hit my leg and backed away. Startled, I jumped backward. Again, it came toward me. I dodged and let it go past. I followed. *Where is it going?* I thought. Tapping it with a paw did not stop it. *Hah. Waste of time.* With that thought, I jumped back on the sofa and went back to sleep. I could hear it wandering about for some time. Eventually the whirring stopped. I opened one eye and saw that it had leashed itself again.

Ash thought it was a cool object. He called it the robotic vacuum cleaner. My next encounter with a similar object scared all the doggy spirits out of me. It happened when we were out charging my Tesla.

AC and DC were very enamored with the Tesla and contemplated buying one. In the family, DC is the car-loving human and AC is the "I want something to take me from A to B" human. I am the "I want a reasonably big place at the back with air conditioning" dog. So there we were, at the showroom, ready to test drive two of them.

I hopped into both the cars and decided that the smaller one was not for me. The space at the back was too cramped. So, the bigger one it was. I heard the man say to DC, "Looks like your dog likes the Model X." The car had huge side doors which opened upwards and unfolded like the wings of a gull (or a hawk, as I thought), allowing me easy access. No stressing out my hips and knees by jumping into the back: I just needed to hop up through the open side door, then wend my way through the individual seats to my place in the back, with its own air-conditioning zone. Easy peasy! I loved it!

DC and I headed out every Sunday morning to charge the car. There were a few office buildings next to the charging station. We would go for a walk along these buildings. It was our Sunday ritual. Wake up—drive to the charger—plug in the car—trot off for the walk—finish with a coffee (for DC). I'm hyper enough without caffeine.

A large building at the end of the road had an eerie feel about it. It raised my hackles every time I walked past. I could sense a presence there, and maybe that explained my instinctive reaction. Bushes about four feet high lined that particular stretch of sidewalk, blocking my view of the driveway on the other side. We used to walk past often, and every time I sensed something but couldn't see, smell, or hear anything. DC would sense my tension. We would look around. *Nothing!* It was very embarrassing.

One day, I picked up the scent of something not alive on the other side of the bushes, along with another, familiar smell. I couldn't place it then. I stopped and froze, head pointing toward the bushes, ears perked, tail stiff. I heard a hissing sound that got louder as it came closer. I scrambled away with my tail between my legs, throwing worried looks over my shoulder at the bushes and the sound beyond.

DC looked at me in surprise. "Zen, what's up, doggy?"

We both peered toward the source of the sound. DC could see over the bushes and had recognized the source of the hissing. I heard a loud guffaw. Hahaha! "Come here and take a look, puppy!"

I was dragged reluctantly into the driveway and the presence revealed itself. It looked like a big blue drum with a light flashing on the top of its rounded head. It was moving on wheels very slowly and making a hissing sound. *Aha! There's the source of that sound*, I thought.

We stopped in front of this object. Grrrr...a low growl was emerging from my throat. The object stopped.

"Zen, meet Mr. Robot," said DC.

My growl finished in a short, sharp, uncertain bark. "Wrroof?"

"Mr. Robot, meet Zen."

Another bark. "WOOF!" Much louder, less fearful and more intimidating, or so I thought. Once the introductions were done, we both went our merry ways. Later I heard DC telling AC, "Zen met a security robot at Microsoft. It was patrolling the grounds. He went nuts. It was so funny. Wish I could have recorded it."

I also managed to identify the familiar smell. In one of my exploratory walks on the farm, I had entered a barn and knocked over a bucket of liquid. The liquid had spilled on my paws. It was sticky and tasted awful. It also had a very strong smell. In panic, I had scrambled out of there. To make things worse, Cathy found red colored paw prints in my bed and wasn't too happy about it. She let me know in no uncertain terms.

The dog park close to our house was very different from the one in Singapore. For one, it was a HUGE fenced-off area. Secondly, most of the dogs there were friendly. Opposite to the entrance, at the far end, was a little grassy patch with a big water tub. We could alternate cooling off in the water and drinking it. The rest of the park was dried mud. A few benches were scattered along the fence for the humans to sit. There was an etiquette to follow when you and your companion entered a dog park. Your human opened the main gate and you both entered a small fenced-off holding area. On the other side, another small gate opened into the main dog park playing area. The "holding area" was for the safe meet and greet. This was where you figured out whether you were welcome in the park. The moment you entered the holding area, all the dogs in the park charged over for a sniff or to bark at you or even worse, to growl at you, a clear sign of, "You are not welcome here," or "I am the big guy here, so don't piss me off." Once all this was established, your walking companion opened the inner gate and let you into a mass of bodies. Now that is scary. Big dog, little dog, noisy dog, friendly dog, all introducing themselves at the same time. You worked your way through this melee and took off. The friendly ones started to follow and a game of Chase Me would begin. The dominant ones would also follow, taking every opportunity to tell you, "This is my turf and I strongly suggest you follow my lead or life will be very unpleasant for you." All this was communicated just by bumping you hard with their shoulders. It was all fine and dandy as long as you did not bump them back. God forbid you bumped them back! It could get ugly very quickly and then the humans had to intervene. The perpetrator invariably got banished from prime time at the park and could only visit when nobody was around.

I made friends with a giant black dog called Oscar. Oscar was ten years old and on my first day, he came over and said, "Welcome to the park, dude. Since you're new here, let me give you a couple of tips. Don't try and play with me. I have OCD and I play only with my Frisbee. Don't touch my Frisbee even if it lands in front of your nose. I don't take that too kindly. Other than that, have a good day!"

"Really? Okay, I will not chase your Frisbee, but is it okay if I chase you?" Since I got no response, I proceeded to do exactly that. Every time Oscar chased the Frisbee, I would chase him. He didn't seem to mind.

The Dish is a small hill on the edge of the Stanford campus. A large satellite dish is perched on top. Hence the name. Dogs are not allowed on the Dish, but they are allowed on a trail that runs along the base of the hill and then goes around the houses. It is fairly long and safe from road traffic. No danger of getting run over by a car. During our walks around there, DC would take off the leash and allow me to run free. In the course of one of these runs, I met Max, an eighteen-month-old dog with an appetite for wood and mud. He would gobble the stuff, giving the impression that his human never fed him. Max's human, Rory, was a scientist working on some unpronounceable subatomic particle research at Stanford. He even walked like one of those particles. Bouncy, jittery, fast—I could see that DC would get breathless just keeping up with him.

Coyotes were spotted on the trail sometimes. I had never seen one till a cold morning in November. DC was out of town and AC's sister and her family were visiting from Austin. AC, AC's nephew, and I were out for our morning walk. We met Max a mile along the trail and started playing our usual chase and bump. I would chase and he would come tearing into me to bump me off my feet. Both of us were full of unbridled energy. It was a crisp morning and the frozen dew crunched under our paws as we ran around.

We were about fifty feet ahead of the human pack. Max suddenly stopped and froze. He was staring at a bush. I followed his gaze and spotted this creature looking at us from behind the plants. It looked like one of us but was slimmer with bigger ears. Max was in full hunting mode: ears pricked...tail erect...muscles tensed. He growled and pounced. Instinctively I followed suit.

The creature bolted out of the bushes, toward the humans, saw them, and veered away toward the other side of the trail. It was quick. Anything that runs, we chase, hunters that we are. Max was ahead of me and we charged down the trail, one black streak and one golden streak.

I heard AC yell, "No, Zen! STOP." The adrenaline was flowing. Primeval hunting instinct overruled any training. In my defense, the magic word "STAY" was not invoked.

We tore around a bend in the trail and...no creature. It had disappeared like a ghost. Both of us sniffed around, found no trace, and lost interest. We quietly trotted back to an excited group of companions. Rory, AC, and nephew were walking up, or rather nephew was running, Rory and AC were walking. I heard Rory say, "That was a coyote. It would be too fast for these two to catch."

Then there was Doogie, my li'l cuz. He came into DC's brother's life because of me. All the males in DC's brother's family love dogs. Ash and Vini desperately wanted one. However, the lady of the house was terrified of anything that had teeth and claws, a familiar theme in DC's extended family. They had grown up in an environment where the only dogs they encountered were street dogs who loved to chase down fearful humans and nip at their heels. Multiple encounters with these dogs had led to a "dog phobia." For many years, AC wouldn't come close to any dog and all dog-owning friends were instructed to keep their pets locked up in the bedroom when AC visited...till Zen Sr. arrived on the scene. He was DC's fortieth birthday gift and to this day nobody can understand why AC, a dog-phobic personality, would gift DC a dog. As it turned out, it was the beginning of a decade-long, no-holds-barred relationship with my species. DC loves to tell this story to anybody who wants to hear it, but I think you all need to hear it from AC.

DC's fortieth birthday was approaching and all my friends were telling me that it is a milestone in your life, like a 25th wedding anniversary. While I was contemplating the gift I needed to get, one of our friends suggested I gift DC a dog. To this day, I don't know what got into me, but I agreed.

DC brought Zen Sr. home one day in April. He was three months old, a little, soft, brown furry bundle of suppressed excitement. I did not want him anywhere near me. What on earth was I thinking when I got DC this present? Dogs are smelly and licky and they can bite, *went the little voice in my head.*

I would put my feet up on the sofa whenever he came to me, so he won't be able to lick them. I also told DC to keep him on the balcony at night. I didn't want this creature peeing and pooing on my expensive carpets. Strangely, Zen Sr. intuitively kept his distance, and though he welcomed me deliriously whenever I came back home, he never jumped on me or licked me. This went on for a month.

One Saturday I was sitting on the sofa and reading my Financial Times. *Zen Sr. was sleeping near my feet. I looked at the sleeping bundle and felt like touching him. I slowly bent over and touched his head. It was so soft—like muslin. He raised his head, looked at me, and went back to sleep. "His head is so soft," I said.*

"So's the rest of him," said DC.

I patted him again and again he raised his head, looked at me quizzically, and then went back to sleep. I felt something. It was not fear. It was a sense of achievement. This one didn't lick or bite. He was cute. With that breakthrough, Zen Sr. kept chipping away at my other fears. One day, he licked my toes. Another revelation. No slobber, nothing wet and dripping, and so soft and gentle. Gradually he wormed his way into my heart. Within a few months of his arrival into our home, he was sleeping in our bed curled up against me. Morning became the best time of my day. He would come back from his walk, jump up on the bed, and gently nuzzle me awake. I was converted! I had got over my phobia. He was my dog.

Unlike my predecessor, I had my own style of bonding with humans, more hands-off but incredibly endearing. I would invite myself for breakfast with Ash and Vini. They convinced their mom to give me some carrots for breakfast. I would accept them from her very gently. No teeth, only lips. As the days went by, any visit to their home was rewarded with precisely three carrots. Apparently, DC had told her that she should not be giving me more than two little carrots. She did not agree! She would call me. I would trot over obediently and gently take them from her hand. In a couple of months, her fear gave way to affection and she would look forward to my arrival for breakfast.

The hunt began in earnest for my clone. According to Ash, their pup had to be a blockheaded, stocky golden English Labrador. A suitable candidate was found after months of intensive searching. Born on a farm outside Oregon, he was lighter in color than me, more white than golden yellow, but he was blockheaded and stocky, just like me, and cute as a peach. He was nameless for a while because his family couldn't agree on a name. The twins wanted to call him Obi-Wan, DC's brother wanted a simpler one or two-syllable name, while the lady of the house preferred an Indian name. So poor cuz was nameless for a good two months after his arrival. They called him Doogie a lot and that name stuck. A rambunctious pup, he plays rough—jumping, bumping, biting my ears hard. As he has grown, the style remains, but now instead of a twenty-pound little furball he is a seventy-five-pound projectile barreling into you. That hurts!

Bedwell Park is a former landfill site converted into a marshland nature reserve. It is a great place to go for off-leash walks. It is aroma heaven for me. Despite being buried, tons of decomposing garbage release gases that only we can smell. On our morning walks, DC allowed me to run around unhindered and free. The only wild animals I had encountered there so far were cackling geese, fast-moving hares, and cautious feral cats. Oh, what a joy to chase them! Early morning at Bedwell was always magical: the sunrise, the solitude, the gentle breeze wafting in from the bay. One of those mornings, however, was not so magical. As was customary, DC and I drove up and parked in our usual spot at the base of a small hill. There are two trails leading to the top of the hill; one is asphalted and winds its way up, while the other is a shorter, steeper walking trail. We meandered up the steep trail and I was about ten feet in front of DC when I noticed a cat-like creature crossing ahead of me.. Since it looked like a cat, I charged at it. I heard DC yell, "ZEN, NO!" I heard the yell but my brain did not process it. I've never understood why both AC and DC always used commands other than STAY. What does NO mean?

I fully expected the creature to scoot away like all cats do. This one, however, turned around, arched its back, put up its tail, and sprayed me with some wet, oily, smelly substance. I took the full blast on my head. It went into my eyes and I inhaled it. My eyes burned and

I gagged on the stench. I tried rubbing my face in the grass, against the wooden fence, just to get the wetness off, but to no avail. All I managed to do was open up a bloody gash on my forehead. It stung like crazy.

While I was helplessly flailing around, snorting, sniffling, and pawing my face, DC caught up with me and hooked up the leash, which had a predictable calming effect. My companion slowly examined my head, face, and eyes and said, "Doggy, you got skunked. Damn. It stinks!"

We completed our walk with me smelling like "I got skunked" and DC keeping a healthy distance from me. By then, I had gotten used to the smell. My eyes had stopped burning and the gash on my forehead had stopped bleeding. On the way home, DC kept all the windows down and allowed me to stick my head out for the entire drive. *Works for me, bro.* We got home and I was banished into the garden. I smelled so bad that DC did not want to let me into the house.

Treatments to remove skunk odor range from home remedies like "soak your dog in tomato juice" to using "Skunk Odor Remover Spray." Luckily AC and DC decided not to turn me into a Bloody Mary but to use the spray first and then give me a head and shoulder bath. Despite their best efforts, the "aroma" did not go away for more than a month. One good outcome from this encounter was that I joined my wild brethren in avoiding skunks. If I spotted something moving in the long grass, I made haste slowly to investigate, and if the object of my curiosity arched its back and presented its butt, I gave it a wide berth.

The new environment with its new stimuli, new experiences, and new people made me into a dog that accepts change easily. In a space of less than a year, I had moved around three continents: from a farm in Australia to an apartment in Singapore and then a house with a backyard (and a fence with a hole) in Palo Alto. As a family, we were learning new behaviors.

I learned to be alone for a few hours without destroying anything.

I learned how to sit quietly in outdoor restaurants. AC's favorite one was PF Chang's at Stanford mall.

I learned how to walk like a good boy in a store. No pulling clothes off the rack in Macys.

I learned to swim. More accurately, I lost my fear of water.

My ancestors came from fishing dogs called St. John's water dogs, which became extinct in the 1980s. They had an obvious fondness for water. I, on the other hand, did not like water, or at least, my first experience with dipping my toes in the warm sea in Singapore was not happy. I ran toward the edge, felt the water touch my paws, and promptly scampered back to dry land. DC was completely befuddled. I could see this speech bubble above his head: *You are a retriever and you don't like water?* I was the antithesis to Zen Sr., who was a complete water puppy. His ultimate pleasure in life was a swim, sometime in the sea, but more often in the condo swimming pool.

This changed with my first trip to the Pacific Ocean. We drove to Pacifica, a small town on Highway 1 with a dog-friendly beach. A dog was romping around on the beach, chasing a ball that his companion was throwing. I whimpered in excitement at the thought of chasing him. When DC unleashed me, I took off like a rocket. We chased each other and on one occasion, my playmate chased a ball into the surf. I blindly followed. Before I knew it, I was neck-deep in the cold ocean waters. There was an instant panic in my brain. Survival instinct kicked in and I started paddling. The humans responded with a chorus of hoots and claps. And so went away my fear of water. From now on, any body of water—lake, pond, sea, fountain—was fair game. AC realized this one day when we were at a friend's house in Atherton. I was playing with Hank, the resident five-year-old doggy, in the backyard, which had a small pond with water lilies. Frank jumped in among the lilies and I followed suit.

There was a horrified scream from Jill (the friend). "Hank, NO! What have you done? Get out of there NOW!"

AC joined the remonstrations: "Zen, NO. OUT! Get out, Zen. BAD BOY!!" Again, no STAY.

Hank ignored her pleas and we splashed around in the pond, among the lilies, the green moss, and the muddy bottom. Slipping and sliding and uprooting the flowers. Finally, Frank jumped out and I followed suit. There we stood, tongues lolling, soaking wet, covered in slimy green, with muddy brown paws but happy faces. Jill and AC stared in horror. Oh, did I forget to mention? I had just been given a bath that morning and to top it all, DC had just got the Tesla detailed.

We were both collared and marched to the garden hose, where all the fun was sprayed off with ice cold water. As the Aussie in me would say, "That was a ripper, mate!"

I also learned that Bordetella—or kennel cough, as it is commonly known—is a nasty infection.

I was in the midst of a very pleasant dream, chasing my buddy Max, when an unpleasant nauseous feeling woke me up. I got out of my Zen Cocoon and stood on the carpet making retching sounds.

AC woke up and turned the light on. "Zen doggy… what's happening, puppy? DC, wake up! Zen wants to throw up. Let him out." Before DC could get out of bed, I retched again and brought up a small portion of undigested kibble. DC eventually opened the door and I ran out into the living room retching. This time, nothing came out. I sat there for a while. DC cleaned up the mess in the bedroom and came out to check on me. I gave him a small tail wag indicating, "I am feeling okay now." We all went back to sleep and I heard DC tell AC, "He seems okay. Must have eaten something on his walk."

The next morning, I almost threw up again. Again, nothing came out. I had an uncomfortable feeling like something was stuck in my throat. By evening, I was feeling sick and unhappy. Every time I tried to bark, I would choke and make this funny honking sound like an agitated goose. It was the same sound I heard those big silly birds make when I chased them in Bedwell Park. *Honk, honk, honk!* and they would fly away. If I got breathless with excitement, the choking and honking fits would start. My throat hurt. I had never felt so miserable in my life.

AC was really worried. "DC, there is something seriously wrong with Zen. Please take him to the vet. He never sounds like this…. Look at him, he is looking so miserable." AC always knows when I am unwell or uncomfortable. It is a spiritual connection between dog and human. The same one that brought me into their lives.

Off we went, to Animal Hospital of Palo Alto, a few minutes' drive away from home. When DC described the symptoms to the vet, I was immediately quarantined in the "cat" examination room. The vet was a gentle old man with a soothing voice and a friendly manner. He examined me and told DC, "Looks like he has kennel cough. Has he been to a dog park recently?" DC replied in the affirmative.

"Maybe that's where he picked up the infection," said the vet. "It is highly contagious and that's why we put you in the cat room. The virus doesn't jump species. It will take two to three weeks to get better. In the meanwhile, no exercise, no playing with any other dog. Avoid contact completely. I will prescribe some antibiotics and something to soothe his throat."

DC asked, "How did he get kennel cough? I thought he was vaccinated against it."

"Well…you know…vaccines are not a hundred percent effective. Maybe this is a mutated virus," said the vet.

Yeah, right, I thought a bit grumpily. *All those injections that you guys keep shooting me up with and they are not even effective.*

The medication helped. In a day my sick feeling had gone, and in the next week the agitated goose had left my body. I was back to my happy, bouncy self. AC, who would wake up every time I had a honking fit, could now sleep peacefully.

Winter season was also holiday season. It is the time humans do not work. Instead, they often travel to meet family or visit fun places.

Having done multiple road trips all over the world, DC always believed that the best way to appreciate the beauty of any country is to drive through it, visit its historical sites, stop and stay in its towns and villages, meet the local people, smile at their idiosyncrasies, experience their hospitality, and eat local food. AC is a fly-over person and not a fan of road trips. So imagine my surprise one evening when I overheard them both planning a road trip.

"We have holidays till January 9th," AC said. "Let's plan a trip somewhere close by with Zen. It'll be fun. We'll get to see how he handles it."

Yay! I thought. *They are planning a road trip and I am going with. How cool is that?*

DC responded, "Yes. We'll also get to see how you handle it."

PART 3

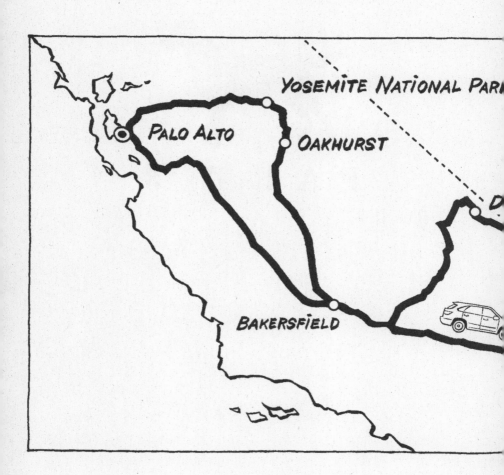

YOSEMITE NATIONAL PARK

PALO ALTO

OAKHURST

BAKERSFIELD

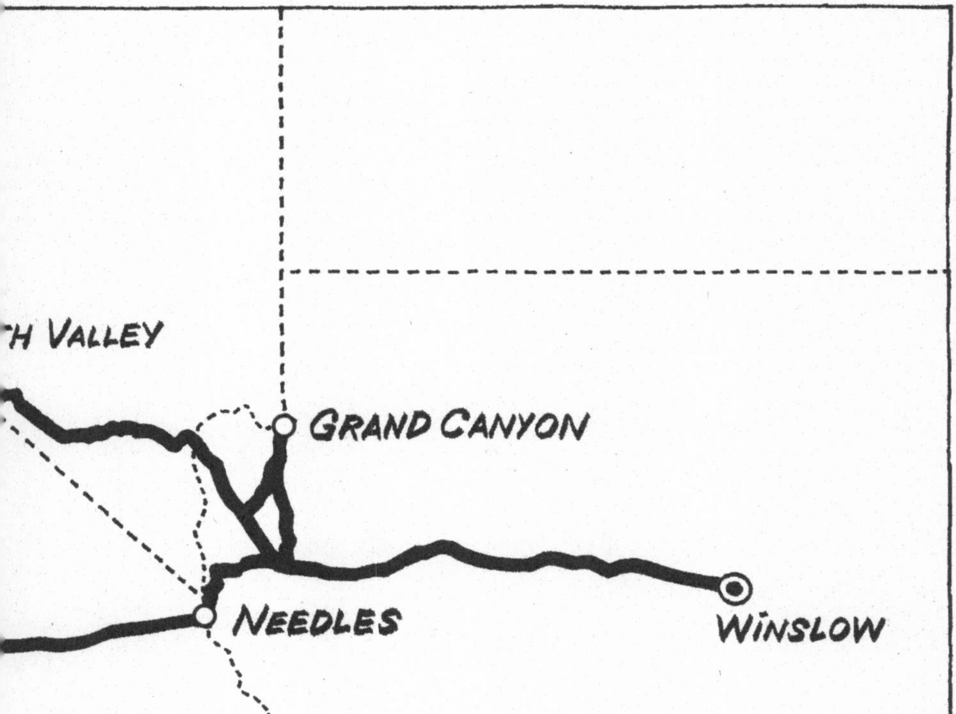

H VALLEY
GRAND CANYON
NEEDLES
WINSLOW

CHAPTER 4

Petrified but Not Afraid

We took two trips to test AC's and my roadworthiness. The first one was a five-day, 400-mile trip to explore Highway 49 and visit Yosemite. The second was a longer one: ten days and 1500 miles to Arizona.

Highway 49 (also known as Golden Chain Highway) is a historic route along the western edge of the Sierra Nevada range in eastern California. It connects all the mining towns of the 1849 Californian Gold Rush. On January 24, 1848, gold was discovered near modern day Sacramento. This find sparked the largest migration in US history. Thousands of people traveled across land and sea, including from far-flung places like China, to mine the gold. The non-native population of California exploded from 880 in March 1848 to almost 100,000 by the end of 1849. These would-be gold miners were called the '49ers. Small mining towns sprung up on the western flank of the Sierra Nevadas. Approximately 200 million dollars' (6.5 billion dollars today) worth of gold was extracted from the ground over a period of three years.

Interesting facts about the Gold Rush

- *Merchants became rich, not the miners, who had to get lucky to strike gold. Merchants provided everything needed to the burgeoning miner population. Levi Strauss was one such merchant. He came to San Francisco in 1850 to make wagon covers and tents. Instead he used the material to make tough pants for the miners, which later became jeans.*
- *The Australian shepherd breed first came into America during the Gold Rush. Demand for mutton and wool increased dramatically during this period. Sheep were imported from Australia and the dogs accompanied them.*
- *San Francisco is built on ships that were abandoned. All the miners who came by sea left their boats behind as they moved inland to prospect for gold. With the city growing rapidly, some ships and boats were repurposed into hotels and shops. Others were sunk in the harbor and over time, the city was built on them.*

DC chose not to take my Tesla for this trip. Instead we had rented a big truck. The space at the back was much larger than in my Tesla. I was a happy puppy. The plan was to drive to Oakhurst, a small town at the southern end of the highway, and then move north with a side trip to Yosemite National Park.

We got our first glimpse of the agricultural belt of California, with its fruit orchards and vegetable farms. Since it was winter time, most of the "farm shops," which are little shacks set up on the road adjacent to the farms, were closed. We arrived at our inn just as the sun was setting. Queen's Inn by the River is a pet-friendly, comfortably rustic collection of rooms by Nelder Creek. As I jumped out the back, the hostess greeted me with a little woof, a huge tail wag, and a hard-to-refuse offer to play. Gracie was young and very agile. Boy, was she a runner! AC unhooked the leash and off we went, careening through the bushes and bounding over potted plants. What a welcome!

My first night away from home was a bit fitful as all of us adjusted to being in a strange room. I was kept awake most of the night with the sounds of wildlife scrabbling around outside, and my unsure little "woofs" kept AC and DC awake as well. The next morning was glorious, bright and sunny. DC and I walked on the trail along the creek, reveling in nature, listening to the calls of the birds just as the sun peeked out. The nip in the air almost caused a Zen Zoomie. The leash kept me in check. I so wanted to play with Gracie, but she was nowhere to be found. *Lazy girl. Must be sleeping,* I thought.

Later in the morning, we headed off to our first sightseeing destination, Bass Lake. Google Maps indicated a fifteen-minute drive to the lake. What we didn't know was that the GPS signal gets very iffy in the mountains. It died on us at a fork and DC took the wrong turn. We realized our mistake when we saw signs for Bass Lake pointing in the opposite direction to where our collective noses were heading. A map at the ranger station was barely readable, not helpful. AC took a unilateral decision to follow the road signs, and after a bit of meandering, we found the lake. DC learned from this and kept a AAA Road Atlas as backup when we were planning our longer cross-country journey later in the summer.

Yosemite is the first national park in the US. Yosemite Falls is also one of the few places in the US where you can see a rainbow at night! It is called a moonbow and it is usually visible on a clear night. Unfiltered light from the moon and stars bounces off the mist created by the waterfall to create the rainbow. Moonbows are most likely to occur in April, May and June.

In Bass Lake, we parked near a collection of buildings called Pines Resort. We got out of the car and began walking toward one of the buildings. There was the aroma of coffee in the air, and knowing DC, we were headed for the source. I meandered along, sniffing the myriad scents in the bushes along the walkway—dog, rat, fish, even a cat. Out of the corner of my eye, I saw a figure. It was standing upright, very still, and looked ready to attack. It was a little shorter than AC. Its mouth was open and I could see the fearsome teeth. AC was standing right next to it.

"OMG!" I barked (we Millennial dogs tend to express some emotions in acronyms). "Watch out, AC! Get back!" I growled warningly at the creature, mustering all the ferocity from the depths of my stomach, hoping to scare it away. It didn't move, and I barked my most imposing, threatening bark. WOOF! WOOF! Again, no movement. *Doesn't it realize that I am a BIG, bad dog who can cause some serious damage? Why isn't it running away?*

Again, I growled and let out another sharp bark. AC and DC were watching me with big smiles. *This is not a joke*, I thought. My nose did not give me any information. There was no animal smell and the figure was not making any sound or moving. I went closer and backed away. *Maybe I'll go at it from a different angle.* So, I crept to the side and... very carefully...strained my neck to take a closer sniff, ready to scramble away at the slightest hint of movement. Anyone watching me would have seen a dog crouching low to the ground, neck extended, nose straining for a sniff, muscles tensed, tail held low...a dog unsure of what it is seeing.

I caught the faint smell of wood and a stronger, familiar aroma: the liquid in the barn and on the robot. I stopped in puzzlement and looked at AC and DC, who by now were laughing loudly. AC was recording this whole event on the phone. *Well,* I thought, *they don't seem to be too scared. Maybe that creature is not dangerous.* I walked up to it...it still hadn't moved...sniffed again... got a stronger smell of wood and the liquid...and walked away. I heard DC ask AC, "Did you get it? So funny! He was growling at a bear statue. Such a clown!"

"Yes, I did," said AC. "Remember how he growled at the Buddha statue back home in Singapore? I had to keep it outside our door so that it wouldn't scare him."

Like some humans have a clown phobia, I have statue phobia. This incident damaged my reputation as the fearless protector of the family.

Highway 49 meanders through small mining towns like Mariposa and Jamestown. We discovered two nuggets near Mariposa: one was a huge gold mass and the other an artisan coffee company. The California State Mining and Mineral Museum houses the largest mass of crystalline gold found during the Gold Rush, a whopping fourteen pounds, mined in 1864.

Further up the road, the aroma of roasting coffee beans announces The Mariposa Coffee Company, a throwback to the gold mining era with a collection of sheds housing a roasting plant and a coffee shop. For DC, this was like entering a candy store.

Even with the windows closed, the aroma of coffee penetrated the car and enveloped us. A bright orange sign announcing "Welcome to Mariposa Coffee Company" greeted us as I drove in and parked the car. I walked to the shop while AC and Zen wandered off to explore the grounds. The shop is a replica of a merchant's store during the Gold Rush—a single story log structure with a sloping roof. A lantern nailed to the beam at the entrance welcomes you. Empty sacks of coffee are strewn around in organized chaos. As I entered the coffee universe, I could see Mariposa Coffee Company's bewildering number of blends stacked in large glass bottles on the shelves. Off to one side was the merchandise: the ceramic cups with

ABHI

the logo, T-shirts, and other small items. All the coffee making equipment was at the far end of the store. In an adjacent room, an old gentleman was happily blending the beans and grinding them for packing.

It was like walking into coffee heaven.. I promptly grabbed a mug and went over to order. After some discussion with the young lady at the counter, I ordered the "Yosemite Dark" blend. The first sip was incredibly gratifying. I wandered around the store in a coffee-induced somnolent state of nirvana. If ever there was heaven on earth, it was right here.

I met the resident pooch, a rather grumpy old dog. DC referred to him as an Australian Shepherd. Memories of my life on the farm in Gatton came flooding back and I wanted to share them, but he was in no mood to listen. Maybe he wasn't born there, so he didn't care. Or maybe he was just old and grumpy and didn't feel like chatting with a young visitor. The coffee shop girl was friendlier than the old dog. Her hands smelled of coffee as she bent down and stroked me under my chin.

Our journey next took us through other gold mining towns like Angel's Camp.

Here's the fun fact about Angel's Camp: it is the only city in the county of Calaveras and is also referred to as the "Home of the Jumping Frog." Jumping frog? Really? In 1865, Mark Twain published a short story called "The Celebrated Jumping Frog of Calaveras County." This

82

story made him famous nationally. Inspired by this story, Calaveras County hosts an annual event, The Calaveras County Fair and Jumping Frog Jubilee. The world record for the longest horizontal jump is 21 feet, 5 3/4 inches, held by the champion frog called "Rosie the Ribiter."

Even I can't jump twenty-one feet and these little suckers can! Bowza!

We got back to Palo Alto for Christmas and a few days later, we were heading to Arizona. The driving distance each day was longer than the earlier trip. That meant I had to spend more time in the back. AC's friends had recommended that we visit Arizona in the winter. It gets really hot down there in summer and yours truly doesn't do too well in the heat.

The plan was to drive to a small town called Winslow via the Grand Canyon and return through Death Valley. The average temperatures forecasted for this trip were in the 40s. This time, DC booked a smaller truck. For some unknown reason, AC didn't like the big one we had for the earlier trip. It turned out to be a huge mistake. The last row was too small for me. I let them know this in no uncertain terms by expressing a reluctance to jump back in and giving them the sad dog look at every opportunity.

It didn't work for them either—heads and the raised tailgate got introduced to each other frequently. This did knock some sense into them, which was useful when they were planning for the Big One later in the summer.

As DC puts it:

Rod and I had been planning to drive down historic Route 66. It is one of the ten "must-do" road trips in America. Our route to Winslow ran through a town called Needles. It also happened to be our first night's halt.

A few historic Route 66 motels are still in operation. However, we chose to stay in the more modern and pet-friendly Best Western. The next morning, Zen and I discovered a conserved 1930s-era gas station called Carty's Station. There were a couple of vintage Ford and Bedford trucks parked in the garage. Standing in front, I let my mind wander to the time this station was a bustling stop on Route 66. Cars driving up and pumping gas. Drivers walking into the single story shack to buy cigarettes and pay for the gas. I love daydreaming. It takes me back to a time when life was simpler and there was so much more to discover on road trips.

The drive from Needles to the Grand Canyon was a revelation. The dry, arid landscape gave way to snow and ice as we climbed from sea level to an elevation of seven thousand feet. Our first view of the canyon was from a viewpoint on South Entrance Road. There was a foot of snow on the walkway next to the car park. Some parts of it were black and slushy. The chilly air sent Zen into raptures. He was a bouncy, happy puppy despite the slush. Let's get back to his narrative....

Dogs, like humans, have temperature preferences. Some like it warm, others like it cold. I was in the latter camp. The slush added to the fun. I stepped in it, splashed around in it, and generally behaved like a badly trained pooch. My paws got black and gooey and I left my prints all over the pristine white snow. This wasn't my first snowy experience. I had gamboled in thick, fresh snow in Yosemite a few days earlier. In the snow, the smells are not as strong. I think the cold air does something to them. I pranced around like a puppy, much to AC and DC's enjoyment. I was happy to be out of the car.

There weren't too many tourists at this time of the year. AC and DC got some excellent views of the canyon. I also tried to get a view by gingerly climbing onto a low wall at the edge and peering into the gorge. Nothing interesting to see, but a few interesting smells did waft up from the canyon.

Our destination, Winslow, is also on Route 66. We were booked in the La Posada Hotel, a historic hotel. La Posada, "the resting place," was the brainchild of Fred Harvey. He was reputed to be the man who "civilized the West" by introducing linen, china, crystal, silverware, and impeccable service to the Santa Fe Railroad. La Posada was Harvey's masterpiece, built in the 1920s at a princely sum of $2 million ($40 million today). It is also a Amtrak railway station.

The property reflects its hacienda heritage. The main block was built by rich Spanish settlers who moved from Mexico in the early 1800s. A huge entrance hall with a massive chandelier greets you as you step through impossibly tiny doors. Off to the left and right are the large residence wings of the hotel. The rooms are named after Hollywood celebrities, Bob Hope, Clark Gable and so on…. We stayed in the Shirley Temple Room. This was in the "new wing," built in the first decade of the twentieth century. A curving staircase led to the second floor. Our room was at the end of the passage. It was outfitted in traditional Navajo colors—deep black, brilliant red, and shining yellow. The carpets were woven with Navajo Indian patterns. Strangely, the bed and the sofa were Victorian. I, of course, got very comfortable on the large bed. Oh! Did I forget to mention, this heritage hotel is totally pet-friendly? There was one little flower garden in the courtyard which said "No Pets Allowed," and understandably so from a human standpoint. They want to smell the roses and not canine bodily fluids! I would take canine bodily fluids over roses any day.

This is where I met Puck, whom DC referred to as "my twin." Our encounter was unexpected and a complete surprise. He was American. I am an Aussie. We probably shared the same great-great-grandfather. This is DC telling the story of the encounter:

The hotel restaurant, The Turquoise Room, is one of the best in Winslow. The food is excellent and a dinner there was highly recommended. Dogs are not allowed inside the restaurant. So they served us dinner in the huge hall to the accompaniment of a pianist.

Post dinner, AC and I walked over to an adjacent smaller hall that had a fireplace. A couple of deep cushion sofas near the fireplace beckoned to us. A log fire was burning away brightly. Zen promptly settled himself next to it. It was warm and cozy. We ordered some wine and ensconced ourselves in the sofas, watching our pup sleeping next to the warmth. He looked at peace with the world, snoring away to glory. Yes, he is the loudest snorer in the family. He had been a trooper through the long day. It had been a 400-mile, twelve-hour journey and must have been exhausting for him. I wish I had his patience and fortitude.

I heard someone say, "Hey, Grandpa, look, there is another Puck!" We both turned to see a teenage girl, long hair in plaits, dressed in jeans with a flowery top and a big smile adorning her freckled face. She was walking up to us, trailed by a balding gentleman.

"Who's Puck?" I asked. Zen opened one eye and looked at the girl.

"He is our dog and he looks exactly like your dog. What's his name?" she said.

"Zen," AC replied.

"Can I say hello?" she asked.

"Of course," both of us said in unison.

"Hi, Zen." She knelt down to cuddle Zen and was promptly rewarded with a sloppy chin lick.

"Where is Puck?" I asked.

"Oh, he is in our room. We were at dinner and left him behind. He has had a long drive," said Grandpa.

"Maybe we can bring him down to meet Zen."

With those words, the young lady took off toward her room. I started chatting with Grandpa.

"Where did you guys drive in from?"

"Today, we drove in from Oklahoma City. Sadie and I are driving over to meet my wife's family in Tucson. Sadie is studying in New York and we live in Bangor. Puck and I drove from Bangor, picked up Sadie, and are heading to Tucson."

"You have driven from Maine?" I said in awe. "Isn't that the other end of the US?"

He smiled. "Yes, it is. We do this trip every year. Only this time, Sadie decided to join me. She is writing a blog on her trip for her school paper."

Just as he finished this sentence, Sadie and Puck came into view. Puck was Zen's identical twin in all respects except the eyes: his were black and Zen's were light brown. He was five years old. The coloring, golden yellow with streaks of white on the shoulders and the stomach, the same block-like head, similar height, the furry wagging tail, the goofy grin...all the same. It was uncanny. If I didn't know Zen was born in Australia, I would have believed he was cloned.

That's all we could see before Zen hurtled over and the two began their play dance. Puck was on a leash, but Zen wasn't and he was all over him. They wrestled while lying down, pawed each other, and gently nibbled each other's ears, tails thumping away happily on the wooden floor. It was pure unadulterated fun. Wish we could play like that, I thought. For me, watching dogs play comes second only to coffee nirvana. The four of us chatted for a while before a very tired-looking Grandpa said he was retiring to bed, as he had an early start the next day. The reunion ended as quickly as it had started, and I remarked to AC, "Isn't this just weird and cool at the same time? Middle of nowhere and we meet Zen's twin."

DC was bundled up, winter coat and gloves and cap. I was wearing nothing other than what I was born in. Nature had given me a winter coat: a soft, fine second layer which I had miraculously grown when winter started. AC had also bought me this cute black fleece from my favorite store in Palo Alto. DC, of course, had forgotten to put it on me. We were on our morning outing in the large backyard which was the pet play area. There were icicles on the grass. My paws were cold and the only way I could stop them from freezing was running around like a maniac. Don't get me wrong, I do like the cold. It evokes a sense of joie de vivre and I express it with my legs. Here comes the Zen Zoomie. I charged around like a dog possessed, with a goofy look on my face, mouth wide open, rump rounded, and tail tucked under me. I heard DC mutter, "It is bloody zero degrees. At least the dog is having fun," whilst taking out the phone and recording my Zoomie.

Later that morning, we drove into Sedona. The popular saying goes, "Sedona winters have just enough nip in them to enhance your cocoa." Sedona should have been called the "healing town" of Arizona. All kinds of karmic healing shops and spas line Main Street, the downtown hangout place. The town is surrounded by red rock formations. The popular ones are called Coffee Pot Rock, Chimney Rock, Bell Rock, and Cathedral Rock. No prizes for guessing how they got their names. The best part of the day, apart from a walk that made my paws go all red, was our late lunch by Oak Creek at the Creekside Inn. The soft burbling of the creek, the outdoor table under an umbrella, and the mountain air (Sedona is at 4,350 feet above sea level) gave AC and DC a very healthy appetite. It was a karmic finish to the day.

Q: What is petrified but not afraid?

A: Petrified Forest National Park. It is about 60 miles east of Winslow. It gets its name from the large deposits of petrified wood rocks that are scattered through the park. Most of the trees and shrubs are from an era 225 million years ago, when they fell, got covered in sediment from lava flows, and were converted into fossils. Over millions of years, tectonic shifts eroded the sediment and the fossils. This has resulted in a landscape that looks like an artist's palette, with colors like desert yellows, muted browns, and resplendent, rich reds.

There are also indications of human habitation. We saw petroglyphs, i.e. images, symbols, or designs carved into the rock by humans, which are thought to be between 600 and 2,000 years old.

Route 66 used to pass through this park. A 1932 Studebaker exhibit marks an old section of it. Adjacent to the Visitor Center is a historic hotel built in the 1920s, Painted Desert Inn. During the '60s it was an oasis on

Route 66. It is built of petrified wood and was once called the "Stone Tree House." We ventured into the tiny cubicle-like rooms and I wondered how small Americans were in those days.

> ## The story of the Harvey Girls
>
> *The Fred Harvey Company recruited women from towns and cities in the East and Midwest to serve customers. These young ladies had to be of a good moral character, have at least an eighth-grade education, display good manners, and be neat and articulate. Their contract stipulated that they could not marry. If hired, the women were given a rail pass to get to their place of employment, a smart uniform, good wages, and room and board. Since their beginning in the 1880s, the Harvey Girls have become American legends.*

I felt sad to say goodbye to such a beautiful place, but the road beckoned, inviting us to step into its serpentine arms. And so, the next morning found us driving from Winslow (elevation 4,850 feet above sea level) to Stovepipe Wells, Death Valley (280 feet below sea level). Our route took us through "Sin City"—Las Vegas. I saw the towering MGM Grand, Bellagio, and the rest of the cityscape through the rear window as it went past at 70 mph. AC and DC decided it was not worth stopping for lunch at the sumptuous buffets in town.

Death Valley National Park: a land of extremes. Snow-clad peaks surround a valley which is the hottest, driest, and lowest place in North America. The highest temperature recorded there is 135 degrees. The area gets only two inches of annual rainfall, and the salt flats of Badwater Basin are 280 feet BELOW sea level. It is the largest national park south of Alaska, with 3.4 million acres or 5,300 square miles. The highest summit in North America, Mount Whitney (14,505 feet), is 85 miles to the northwest. What a study in contrast!

Who would name a national park "Death Valley"? We attended a ranger talk at the Visitor Center. He asked the question and then proceeded to tell us the rest of the story.

Let's roll back in time to 1849, when gold was discovered in California: an era which yielded fairytale stories of rags to riches, a time which gave birth to legends of despair like the "Lost Forty-Niners." Lured by the promise of riches in the west, people from the more populated East Coast migrated in large numbers. They had to cross the Sierra Nevadas to get to the gold. Remember the Golden Chain Highway and all the gold mining towns? That's where the wagon trains were headed. Salt Lake City was a jumping off point for the journey to California. For safety reasons, groups of wagons got together to form a "wagon train." Common sense indicated that they had to cross the mountains before winter set in and snow closed the trails. One wagon train did not get that memo and greed overcame common sense, leading to disaster. They set out in October 1849 along an established trail called the Old Spanish Trail. The going was slow and hard. The fear of being stranded in winter led some members of the train to explore a potentially faster route which went through what is now called Death Valley. A guide armed with a hand-drawn map of the faster route convinced them to follow him. After a few days of slow pace, two groups, the Bennett-Arcan group and the Jaywalkers, further split from the main wagon train. They reached what is now called Furnace Creek, in Death Valley, on Christmas Eve of 1849. To the west, they could see a mountain range. Here they were, freezing in the cold, oxen starving, and wagons beat up and busted. Their choices were almost Hobsonian: stay and definitely die of cold, or try to cross the mountains into California and potentially survive to strike gold. The Bennett-Arcan party decided to cross the mountains across a pass they could see. They were unsuccessful and had to come back down into the valley. Two members of their group, William Manly and John Rogers, went off to seek help. They trekked 250 miles across the Mojave Desert to Rancho San Fernando near Los Angeles. More than a month later, they returned to the few surviving members of the group with food and mules. Rogers and Manly then guided the survivors to civilization.

"Just as we were ready to leave and return to camp we took off our hats, and then overlooking the scene of so much trial, suffering and death spoke the thought uppermost saying: 'Good bye Death Valley!'" – William Manly

We had decided to stay in a small place called Stovepipe Wells. The name evokes an image of a well with a stovepipe on it. It's partially true. During the mining boom in the late nineteenth century, the wells were two water holes dug into the sand. This was the only watering place in the valley. A stovepipe was used as a marker because sand obscured the spot. Rising out of the mid-afternoon haze in the middle of Death Valley, Stovepipe Wells is a slightly modern version of a nineteenth century town. The small ranger station, built out of roughly hewn wood and painted light green with a dark green sloping roof, greets you as you enter the settlement. An ancient fire truck is parked across from the station. It is painted red and other than the flat tires is otherwise well preserved by the ultra-dry air. Our motel/hotel, Stovepipe Wells Village Hotel, could have passed for military barracks. Painted in the same colors as the ranger station, it was simple but charming. The service staff were friendly and I was given a warm welcome. A small grocery store opposite the hotel provided the only shopping in town!

Despite its name, Death Valley's stark scenery attracts millions of visitors every year. Some of the more accessible attractions are the Badwater Basin, a huge salt lake, the Artist's Drive, and the Artist's Palette. Dogs are not allowed on any non-tarmac area, which is pretty much the whole of Death Valley, so I was left to stew in the back of the car as AC and DC followed their tour guide ranger to the salt lake. Lucky it was winter time and it wasn't hot, or else moi would have been cooked and turned into a chocolate-colored Lab. The only place I could hop out of the car was in the Mesquite Sand Dunes and that because AC (usually the one to stretch the rules, and thus referred to as the Amenable Companion) took me 15 feet onto a dune. The sand was so soft and cushiony that it felt like walking on a cloud.

Natural Mystery in Death Valley

The Racetrack is one of the most mysterious attractions in Death Valley. It is accessible only with a four-wheel-drive truck, and hardcore off-roaders carry spare tires because they expect to have at least one blowout. The razor-sharp gravel is capable of shredding tires. The area is a mud bed that has rocks of all sizes with long tracks trailing behind them as if pushed by a paranormal hand. Some of the tracks are 1500 feet long.

How are these heavy rocks moving? What explains the tracks?

This mystery confounded geologists for years till one of them decided to use time-lapse photography to solve it. During winter, the miniscule amount of water deposited on the mud bed freezes. High winds slide the rocks along the ice, which then melts, leaving behind the tracks. Hence the name "Racetrack."

Our drive back home was long and boring and wet. After years of drought, California was experiencing heavy rains. An SMS alert for flooding near our house in Palo Alto caused a minor panic in the front of the car. One phone call to DC's bro reassured my humans that all was well. Nothing to worry about. We reached home high and dry.

Within three months of our arrival in California, we had visited five national parks and driven 2,500 miles. We had retraced the footsteps of the forty-niners and driven with the road warriors on Route 66. We had met amazing people and even more amazing dogs.

We all learned a few things during this trip:

1. I can do road travel without throwing up in the back of the car. I needed to be out of the car every two hours or so.
2. I can stay in a different motel every night and still sleep like a puppy. I became inured to strange noises in the night.

3. I was always accorded a warm welcome—in hotels, national parks, cafes, even a spa.

4. AC and DC can be with each other 24/7 and still be talking to each other. Coffee and its hold over DC is a source of conflict. But they seemed to have worked through it in these trips. There is a cadence to the relationship which I will describe later.

Little did I know that this road trip was the beginning of our cultural and historical immersion into the US. That genie was out of the bottle and it held untold surprises. I was going to write my own version of Steinbeck's *Travels with Charley: In Search of America*. Published in 1962, it is a travelogue of a cross-country road trip that Steinbeck undertook in 1960 with his canine companion, a poodle called Charley. In his own words, *"I had not heard the speech of America, smelled the grass and trees and sewage, seen its hills and water, its color and quality of light... So it was that I determined to look again, to try to rediscover this monster land."*

Like Steinbeck, I wanted to discover the riches of this monster land.

PART 4

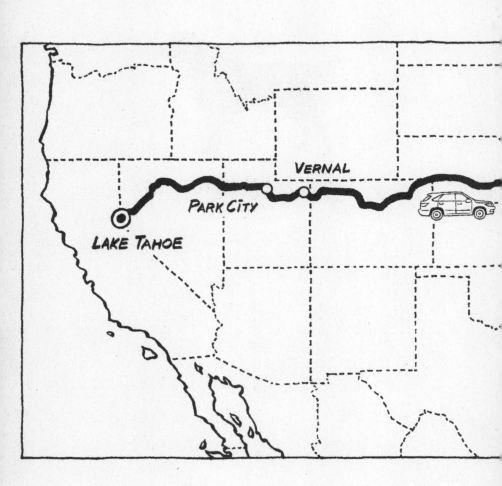

VERNAL

PARK CITY

LAKE TAHOE

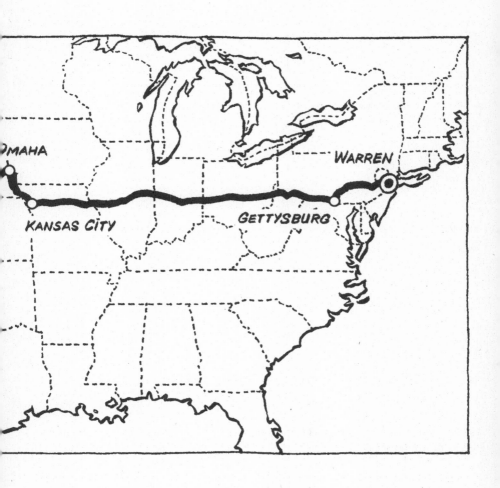

CHAPTER 5

The Odyssey That Began with a Splash

*O*n my work trips, I always flew over most of America. The longest drive I ever did was from Columbus, Ohio to Lexington, Kentucky. It was winter and a bit dangerous because of black ice. The scenery was breathtaking—the pristine white landscape broken in places by picket fences, the naked trees sticking out of the snow in protest. I struggled to keep my eye on the road. I promised myself then: a road trip across America had to be on my bucket list. There was no better way to enjoy American small-town hospitality, its culture, its natural beauty, and its people.

Surprisingly, the suggestion to undertake a trip of this magnitude came from AC. Emboldened by our winter trips, the ever practical and logical AC had a compelling argument. Firstly, it would be summer, when the days are long and the weather is hospitable. Stanford would be closed for the summer. Secondly, our lease for the house was ending on the 30th of June and we had no intention of renewing. We had to move house anyway. So, why not move into a car for two months, return in September, and sign a fresh lease in a new place? Finally, time was not on our side. We were returning to Singapore at the end of the year, so we had only one summer. It was now or never. Not that I needed a compelling argument to take a road trip. I began the planning for the journey.

The most important part was the route. With a limited knowledge of America, I referred to various blogs, books, and websites to decide which places were to be visited. Selection of the route was based on a few criteria, born from the experience of our earlier trips.

1. Never drive more than 500 miles in a day. That was the maximum distance we could drive without feeling exhausted. On the Arizona trip, we would stop every two hours to let Zen stretch his legs and do his job. We had averaged 50 mph with all the rest stops and food stops. A 500-mile drive roughly translated to a 10- to 11-hour daily journey. An added benefit was that the long summer days meant we never drove in the dark.

2. Do not drive every day. This rule would give us at least one day and two nights in a town. The idea was to experience and enjoy the sights, sounds, food, and dog parks of the place that we were visiting.

3. *Never travel the same route twice. We had decided that Maine would be our easternmost destination. We had to see if the state was full of Zen clones. This rule meant our route to Maine had to be different from the one back home.*

4. *Minimize interstate expressway travel. The journey was the objective. Getting from point A to point B as fast as you can was not. The more meandering, the better. We got lost a few times and took a few unplanned detours, as you will read later. All of it was not necessarily fun, and sometimes it ended with arguments with AC. These got settled quickly, because Zen would pop up in the back seat when we started arguing. He had the patient doggy look that said, "Hey guys, what are you going on about? It's a fun trip. Stop it and enjoy the drive. I am." It usually worked.*

Multiple options were discussed and debated. One option was to go through the southern states, then follow the Atlantic coast to New England and return though the northern states. This one was dropped because it gets very hot in summer in the South. As a result, we cut all the southern states from the planning. Another option was to drive to Seattle, then cut across the north all the way to Maine and return through the middle. Unfortunately it is hot in Kansas and Nebraska in August. Hence this option was also nixed. Finally we decided to go through the middle and come back through the north.

The plan was to break up the trip into three legs. Leg 1 was Palo Alto to Warren, New Jersey. Leg 2 was New England, New York, and back to Warren. Leg 3 was Warren to Palo Alto.

Google Maps was the favored planning tool. Pet-friendly hotels/motels and Airbnbs were booked for the first four stops. Why did I book the first four stops and not the rest? I don't know. Maybe boredom set in, or maybe I just wanted to go with the flow. As it turned out, two of them were a disaster. That didn't go down well with AC, who then took on the responsibility of booking the accommodation. More on that later.

The next decision was about the car. My Tesla was not the ideal vehicle for this trip, so DC swapped it for a cousin's Acura MDX. It was black and beautiful. comfortable, quiet, and not too high for me to jump in (the only requirement AC had for the car). AC and DC tested the height of the raised tailgate, their last experience with one having been painful. It passed the height test. Using my French language skills, I named it Beauté Noir (Black Beauty). The car had 80,000 miles on it, but DC was assured that it was reliable. Beauté Noire did not miss a beat through the entire 10,000-mile journey. The cousin was only too pleased with the swap.

We also had to plan the number of bags that went into the car. There were a few "must go into the car" items, mostly mine—two different types of food, two bowls, toys (my favorite singing monkey provided some entertainment in Maine), chew bones, treats, leash, harness, collar, wet wipes, sleeping mattress, and first aid kit (which would be useful in Custer). AC and DC had their usual clothes, shoes, snacks, and the unusual two pillows. The therapeutic pillows were a must after DC had torn a back ligament sleeping on a bad hotel pillow a few years ago. Everything else was optional.

T -7 days. A huge metal container, called a PODS unit, was deposited in our driveway. All our stuff was going into it for two months, except what we were planning to carry with us in the car. The Zen Cocoon was also going into the container. It was too big to fit into the car. I had learned that I could sleep without it, albeit not as soundly. A small sacrifice to make for the many pleasures that awaited us over the next two months.

T -1 day. A flurry of packing activity took place. Like the last time in Singapore, things disappeared and never came back. My favorite carpet went away despite my best efforts to keep it. I even tried to sit on it to stop them from taking it. Alas, I was unsuccessful. Rolls with plastic, newspaper, and bags littered all the rooms in the house. The only clutter-free space was my sofa. I heard lots of debate and arguments about what was going into the PODS container. Dishwashing liquid? PODS or throw. What about the wet, stinking carpet from the garage? Keep or throw? Can we donate this chair to Goodwill? Where is the TV going? There was nonstop noise and action. The arguments were like a sonata, the low mumbles of disagreement (usually DC), the rising note of irritation (usually AC), followed by the sigh of resignation, depending on who had started the argument and who was resigned to the decision. I kept my furry mouth shut and stayed away, except where it involved my toys or my sleeping gear. Anytime a toy was touched, I promptly grabbed it and ran off. If someone touched my mattress, I flopped on it, making it difficult to take away. I don't like to move. Despite all my relocations, I am still uncomfortable with moving. DC packed my stuff sneakily, when I was away on my walk.

D-Day. Two very large men showed up and helped load the PODS container, which subsequently was taken to a storage yard. I was sent away to Ash's house for the day. The stuff going with us on the road trip was put in the car. Everything else that didn't qualify for PODS or the car was either donated or dumped into the trash. DC's bro was the lucky recipient of all the alcohol and food. The back seat of Beauté Noire was packed so high that I could barely see my companions seated in the front. I am sure DC could see nothing in the rearview mirror. Was that going to be dangerous?

The house was empty, the car was packed, and we were ready to go. I got into the driver's seat and started the car. It was evening. Our day had been exhausting, both physically and mentally. I was looking forward to a relaxed evening with Rod and Isa in Orinda. We were going to spend the night there. A short time earlier, Ash and Vini had bid Zen an emotional farewell with lots of tears, hugs, and cuddles. As I eased onto the 101, thoughts kept tumbling through my head. We have taken the plunge. I hope the trip goes well. What if we have a breakdown in the middle of nowhere? Is the AAA number handy? What if Zen falls sick? A hundred what-ifs. I can see that AC is apprehensive about the road trip. *Now, there was no turning back. We had cut the proverbial cord, and if we aborted the plan, we would have to live out of a car for the near future. I couldn't see Zen behind all the bags. I thought,* Isn't it great that dogs live in the present? *I am sure he was happy that his food, his toys, his mattress, and his companions were with him, in that order.*

We left Rod and Isa's house the next day, refreshed after a relaxed morning. Our first stop was Lake Tahoe. As the age-old military adage goes, "No plan survives its first contact with the enemy." Neither did ours. We had chosen to begin our trip on the July 4th weekend, an amateur mistake. One that only a non-American visitor can make. For most Americans, a long weekend is an invitation to get out and go somewhere. There were hundreds of cars headed to Lake Tahoe and we crawled our way to Tahoe City in five hours, a journey that should have taken us no more than three.

Tamarack Lodge Motel is just beyond Tahoe City on the western shore of Lake Tahoe. The property had a two-story building with rooms and ten independent cabins. It had a rustic feel to it. More importantly, it was pet friendly with a resident black kindred soul. Our cabin was the farthest away from the parking area, in a secluded spot. Scampering sounds and owl hoots kept me awake all night. *This is not a good beginning*, I thought. Despite that, I woke up to the crisp Tahoe air all bushy tailed and bright eyed, ready for my morning walk. By the way, most days I wake up bushy tailed and bright eyed. It is the humans who wake up grumpy!

We walked into the forest behind our cabin and kept an eagle eye out for bears and coyotes. Burton State Park adjoins the motel and we were warned about the wildlife. Didn't see any, though. After an uneventful walk and with my brunch done, I was snoozing near the window when I saw Mochi, a one-year-old brother of mixed parentage.

Hey, let me out! I wanna go say hi. Please, pretty please. I begged AC, who opened the door, and I shot out to say hello to Mochi. We introduced ourselves and began playing. We pranced around and splashed in the little muddy stream running outside our cabin. We chased each other through the trees. It was fun. Once playtime was over, we were wet and dirty and happy. A hose-down was essential. While I took the hosing down obediently, Mochi did not. He obviously did not like water. When the first cold drops landed on his back, he wriggled out of his human's grasp and scooted away. What followed was a game of hide and seek, Mochi tearing through the compound and his companion chasing him with his voice rising on an exponential octave curve.

"Mochi! Come back here, Mochi! MOCHI, STOP! COME HERE NOW!"

Sigh! Mochi's companion was going about this the wrong way. Any half-decent dog trainer will tell you that you never chase a dog. We have this unique ability to convert a chase into a game of catch-me-if-you-can. That's how we play. The game ended when DC collared Mochi, who was then given a hosing down despite his vigorous protestations.

That's how the day began. Very exciting for me. I thought, *If this is what every day looks like, I am going to enjoy this trip a lot.*

We braved another monster traffic jam on our way to the Tallac Historic Site, twenty five miles south. Oh boy! DC had really screwed this one up. This was where the rich and famous built their summer estates in the 1800s and the 1900s. The estates owned by three families, Pope, Baldwin, and Valhalla, have been preserved as a source of envy for the modern generation. Visitors can see how the Pope family lived and entertained in their mansion. One cool feature is its barking dog kitchen door. Bears abounded in those days and the more intrepid ones tended to sneak into the kitchen to grab food. Easy pickings! The Popes rigged an alarm. Opening the kitchen door would trigger a loud series of WOOFs, thereby frightening the bear away.

Ducking through the legs of the teeming hordes on the shores of the lake, I was allowed to dip my paws into the water. It was cleaner than the muddy stream I had jumped into with Mochi, but boy, was it cold! I scampered out in a few seconds. Lake Tahoe is the second deepest lake in the United States, measured at 1600 feet. Wonder what lives deep down there?

DC, forever on a coffee prowl, discovered a gem of a cafe, Tahoe House Bakery and Gourmet Cafe. It is dog-friendly, a bit Old World with a selection of homemade pies and cakes and of course, great coffee. As you all know, DC can never resist a good coffee. The smell triggers an animal instinct, a kind of a Pavlovian response, which screams, "I have to go in and drink a cup." A bit like me in that regard. Food-motivated and willing to do anything just for a taste.

The cafe had a patch of artificial lawn near the seating with a ring hammered into the wall. The sign said "Dog Parking." AC and DC found it positively hilarious. I thought it was discriminatory, albeit Instagram-worthy. Despite my mortification, they took a photo with my butt parked.

CHAPTER 6

Pets Welcome, Children Must Be on a Leash

It got hotter as we crossed into Utah from Nevada, leaving behind lush forests and the aquamarine Lake Tahoe. I was looking out the window and saw a vast shimmering surface. The sea! Water!

Can I get out and play in the water? I let out an excited whine. I have different whines: a low-intensity one that rises and drops, then rises again, forms my excited one. Another one, my "Help me" whine, is soft and intermittent, normally used when I am on the wrong side of a door. Lastly, I have a short, high-pitched yelp that sounds like a "Yip" when my toes get stepped on, which DC does with amazing regularity.

AC and DC couldn't understand what the fuss was about till they glanced outside and DC said, "Look, the whole area is shimmering like the surface of a lake. Maybe Zen thinks it is water. I think he wants to play in there."

Another excited whine.

"Sorry, buddy. It's not water. Can't play there," was the response.

The I-80 cuts through the Bonneville Salt Flats, a dazzling white plain resembling an alien world. The shimmering hot air raised a mirage of a lake surface. It is an endless stretch of nothing, stark white desert, thirty thousand acres of sheer desolation. Not a single bush or tree in sight. Nothing grows here because of the harsh, salty environment.

A flat piece of land that stretches for miles on end with a surface that is as firm as concrete makes it a godsend for straight-line speed demons. Land speed records are routinely broken on the Bonneville Speedway. The latest record stands at 485 mph. Bowza! That's as fast as a small plane.

The highway runs straight as an arrow for a hundred miles east of Wendover. This stretch is known as the "Wendover death strip." The drive is so monotonous that drivers doze off at the wheel, often with fatal consequences. Somewhere on this stretch, I heard DC say to nobody in particular, "I just saw a sign advising drivers to calibrate their speedometers using the speed measuring marks." DC did that a lot, talk to nobody. Maybe it was a way of warding off sleep. Usually, AC would be listening to an audiobook with earphones and was deaf to DC's comments. I heard DC grunt and a few moments later, a short "Yes." The speedometer test was done. DC concluded that the error between the recorded speed and the speed shown on the speedometer was only 1.5%. AC wasn't listening.

Earlier in the morning, another DC comment dropped in the car. "Look, a sign that says **DO NOT PICK UP HITCHHIKERS.** That's strange. Why would you put that in the middle of nowhere?" The answer soon revealed itself. An exit sign read: **Exit - Lovelock Correctional Facility.** That's the politically correct name for a prison. Lovelock was O.J. Simpson's residence for a few years. Simpson, an ex-NFL star, was prosecuted for murdering his wife and her lover. He was acquitted for the murders but was convicted later for burglary. And we definitely did not pick up any hitchhikers.

Park City is about forty-five miles southeast of Salt Lake City in the mountains. It hosted the 2002 Winter Olympics. Fondly referred to as Bark City, it is known to be one of the friendliest cities in the world for my kind. Sydney, a friend whom we had agreed to meet up with later in the trip, had suggested staying there instead of Salt Lake City and boy, was she right. Her words had been, "Unless you are a Mormon, you have no business staying in Salt Lake. Park City is prettier and less crowded." Heeding her advice, we checked into the

Best Western. I got a warm and welcoming cuddle from the lady at reception. The room was big and comfortable and soundproof.

We had a view of the Olympic Park and the magnificent ski jump from our window. Park City is cute and charming, with one of the best dog parks that I have ever visited. AC found it on Yelp, where it had a well-deserved 5-star rating. It was huge and amazingly scenic. The soft green turf made it a pleasure to play and chase other dogs. It also had a big natural pond that served as the dog pool. Bowzaa! One fellow visitor was splashing around in there. I wasn't allowed in. I think my humans didn't want to bathe and dry me at the end of a long day.

Park City was once a silver mining town, and many buildings on Main Street are preserved to reflect the city's heritage. The shops and restaurants were festooned with celebratory stars and stripes banners and announcements of special sales for the Fourth of July celebration. All the shops were welcoming and allowed me in. The ladies (two-legged and four-legged) loved me. One shop even had this endearing sign: "Pets welcome, children must be on a leash." Way to go, Bark City.

We rounded off the day watching the fireworks from a hilltop just outside our (ahem) kennel. The fireworks dazzled and danced against the backdrop of a clear night sky. It was a fitting and spectacular farewell to my 'favoritest' city in the world.

CHAPTER 7

The Mystery of the Missing Cats

At 0945 hours, we departed Bark City for Denver. There was a boring route and a scenic route. AC and DC decided to opt for the latter. We were on a driving holiday, after all! The whole point is not to go from A to B directly but explore A1, A2, and A3 before arriving at B. Of course, some of the exploration happens due to navigational errors and some of it because of GPS misdirection. Google Maps orders you to go down the small country roads, partially paved roads, and all kind of trails just because it makes the trip shorter. All in all, it was a long driving day through some of the most scenic routes in the country: at least two national parks, lovely valleys and towering mountains, and picturesque towns nestling in the turns of the Colorado River. We drove through a bunch of small towns—Roosevelt, Duschesne, Vernal, and of course the top ski resorts of the Rockies such as Vail, Eagle, Avon, and Aspen.

Just outside of Vernal, we visited the Dinosaur National Monument Park. The main exhibit was a wall of dinosaur bones at the Dinosaur Quarry Exhibit Hall. The poor animals died near a river 150 million years ago. Over millennia the bones that were buried in the river beds turned into rock, like the wood in the Petrified National Park. The tectonic action of the continental plates (did I just say that? My canine IQ rocks. Bowzaa!) pushed them to the surface. Now tourists can touch these bones freely. I could not sniff them or chew them, since dogs are not allowed in the hall. AC hadn't yet got the "whisper the magic word in the reception lady's ear" formula quite right. It would be perfected by the time we reached New England. So, I had to cool my paws in the air-conditioned comfort of the car while AC and DC huffed and puffed their way through the 100-degree heat of Dinoland. We stopped for lunch at a charming cafe called Bedrock Depot in a town called Dinosaur. They had some interesting items on the menu. A "Stegosaurus veggie roll" (do you see the irony in that?) and an "Allosaurus burger" alongside others like the "BLT sandwich." The burger tasted of beef. DC gave me a bite.

The fun part of the trip came after lunch as we drove along the Colorado River. At one point, we stopped for a break. AC snuck me out of the car so I could dip my paws and splash in the river. Yippee dipee doo! I have an abiding love for all kinds of water: sea, lake, river, stream, puddle—it beckons me like the sirens in Greek lore.

Downtown Denver, La Quinta: a pet-friendly motel chain, also the first and only place we cancelled after one night. We were given a ground floor room at the far end of the building. By now, we had figured out how to be more efficient with our luggage. After lugging it up and down a flight of stairs in Park City, AC, the efficient one, had decided that we should leave the big duffels in the car. A small bag with enough clothes to last a couple of days and toiletries, plus one bag with my food and bowls and my sleeping gear, would be taken to the room. In case we missed taking something, Beauté Noire was parked just outside the door. We could keep an eye on him through the cracks in the door. I am not kidding. It looked like the motel operator had decided to fit a plank in place of the door. To make matters worse, the bed linen was stained and the bathroom was grimy. The last words I heard before I fell asleep were in AC's no-nonsense tone: "I don't want to stay here. We should check out in the morning. From now on, I will do all our hotel bookings." And so, the next morning we packed our belongings into Beauté Noire and headed toward Broomsfield, midway between Denver and Boulder. AC's research had thrown up a beautiful resort called Omni Interlocken. It was pet friendly and had a large pool and an 18-hole golf course adjoining the property. Our "mountain-view" room on a high floor did not disappoint. The large windows opened to a breathtaking view of the Rockies. I loved it. Video evidence shows me with my forepaws perched on the window sill, looking out and wagging my tail happily.

Denver is called the "mile high city"—the fifteenth step of the Denver City Hall is exactly one mile, 5,280 feet, above sea level.

Boulder is a small university town about an hour northeast of Denver. The main street of downtown Boulder meanders into the hills after a few blocks of shops and restaurants.

Why were we headed for the hills?

We had a dinner date with a friend from Stanford, Sydney, and her husband, Tom. They lived in the hills outside Boulder. I had met Sydney in Stanford earlier. She was a calm and affectionate personality. Her tone was different, slow, tender like her touch, not the one I usually heard in Palo Alto. She smelled of nature, the woods, the flowers. Tom, her husband, was a tall man. He had a very friendly voice and he spoke in a measured tone with a smile behind it. He exuded doggy love and so I paid special attention to him the whole evening.

Sydney had emailed driving instructions to AC. They were probably typical for a person who lives there. She herself admitted, "I use my phone to talk. I don't know how to use WhatsApp or read email on the phone."

AC read them out to DC. "Drive up 36 and take the Boulder Canyon exit. Hang left at the exit and keep going for a couple of miles till you see a sign that says Sunshine Canyon Road. Turn right at the sign and after about four miles you will come over a hill. About a hundred yards down the other side, you will see a bunch of mailboxes. Next to the mailboxes is a dirt road. Keep coming down the lower part of that road. Don't go up the slope, or else you will be in a different house. You will see my car, a Volvo, and Tom's truck. Our house is just there. It is 8300, Sunshine Road. We don't get a cell signal here. Here's my landline. Call me if you get lost. See you at 6:30 PM."

I was wondering how either AC or DC was going to call her if there was no cell reception. Not for me to figure out. Cross the bridge when you come to it.

We blew past the mailboxes a few times and had to execute a couple of tight U-turns. Eventually, we got there in fading light.

Our host's house was stunning. It was modeled on a Swiss chalet with a high, sloping roof and a huge main door. At the back was a large cantilevered patio deck with the barbecue and an outdoor dining table. As you stood on the patio, the only sound you heard was the wind rustling through the leaves and the only sight you saw was the magnificent vista of the sun setting behind the mountains, bathing the sky in hues of red and orange. The house had been featured in *Playboy*. The previous owner was a bachelor who had outfitted it to suit his lifestyle. Then he got married and discovered that his wife was afraid of deer. So, he had to sell the house. Tom and Sydney bought it but Tom could not enjoy the bachelor pad features. As he ruefully admits, "Sydney made me take them all out."

"This is fantastic," said AC as they settled down for dinner. "You guys have a lovely home."

"Yes. We love it and will stay here even though it is a bit away from the University and there is no cell connection," said Tom. "We've got internet and Amazon doesn't have a problem finding this place. It's getting tougher to bike into town and back, though. The hill seems to have become higher over the past couple of years," he continued smilingly.

"That's why I am telling him that we need a place in town," Sydney piped in. "He stays here alone when I am over at Stanford and I worry that he is going to fall off his bike one day or have a heart attack climbing the slope."

"How come you don't have a dog?" asked DC. "You have the perfect house."

"We have had twelve cats," Tom said. "Some of them disappeared over the years." He sounded like he missed them but not like he really missed them. I did not think he was really a cat man.

"Disappeared?" DC asked with a quizzical look.

"Yeah. Don't know how," he continued, "A couple of them disappeared when we were not at home. They were adopted, so we figured that they took their affection somewhere else. A few years later, another one went out for its morning stroll and never came back. The strangest one, though, was Molly. She was an indoor cat. We got her as a kitten. She was quite shy and would hide under the bed in our room when we had guests. I never recall her going beyond the steps in the front. A few weeks ago, she was snoozing in the bench by the front door when I went out for a run. When I came back, she wasn't there, so I figured she might be inside the house. We looked all over the house, but never found her."

By now, AC and DC were a little worried. Tom, the consummate storyteller, was in full flow. He was having fun. We were still sitting in the patio and the only light on the table was from a large candle flickering in the night breeze, casting eerie shadows on the deck.

Casually, Tom remarked, "Mountain lions probably got them."

There was a sharp intake of breath and AC said, "You have mountain lions here?"

"Yeah. I opened my front door one morning and there he was. Standing on the steps. Probably hunting the cat."

"Did he get it? The cat?"

"Nope. The cat was fine. I must have scared him away," said Tom.

DC was peering into the darkness nervously. "Have they come up here any time?"

"No. They keep away from humans. I've seen only that one in the last ten years." I heard a relieved sigh from DC.

When dinner was over and we were getting ready to depart, DC called out, "Zen. Come on. Let's go." I trotted out into the dark and DC just stood there watching, didn't follow me out. I know why...fodder for a mountain lion. So much for loyalty and companionship!

My intrepid companions decided to spend a day visiting Rocky Mountain National Park. We took a leisurely drive on Trail Ridge Road, which starts at the entrance to the park and winds its way up to 12,000 feet, the highest point in the park. The windows were down and a potpourri of smells entered the car as the environment changed. Temperate to sub-alpine. Aspens gave way to firs. At some point, we emerged above the tree line. It was bright and very windy, but not hot. Barren hills stretched out in front of us. The temperature dropped like a rock. I didn't feel cold. I have one God-given layer of fur—okay, I have an inner layer that I will shed in the summer, so I may have two God-given layers. My humans were freezing and scrambled to extract their jackets. There were a few patches of snow in the higher altitudes, and I got to play in one. The yin of the warm summer sun and the yang of the cold snow set me off. Zen Zoomie time… Alas, I was on a leash. I did a low key version of the Zoomie. It's tough to do high speed U-turns on snow and ice.

The area is so gorgeous that I fell in love with it. I declared that I was available for short-term adoption/holidays with any family, rancher, horse, or elk that has a primary residence in the Rockies. I thought Bark City was great. This was even better.

Onward tomorrow to Omaha, the home of the Oracle of Omaha, Warren Buffett.

CHAPTER 8

A Failed but Legendary Startup in 1860

Today I did not feel that good. I did not know what it was. I was restless and kept fidgeting around in the back, panting like I had climbed a mountain. Dogs pant when stressed. I usually can be very stoic. But today was different. Something was bothering me.

On a warm sunny morning, we left behind my spiritual home, the Rockies, and headed into the vast prairie of eastern Colorado and Nebraska. It was another long drive of 500 miles. Sigh! Another twelve hours in the back. DC has zero planning skills. I could do better. However, the long drive was not the cause of my discomfort.

AC remembers,

I was worried. I could hear Zen panting and fidgeting in the back. My sixth sense was tingling. From the first day that we brought Zen home, I've had a special connection with him. I always knew when he was disturbed or unhappy or hurt.

"Zen seems uncomfortable. Why is he so restless? He sounds stressed. Maybe his bed has shifted. Let's pull over and check," I said.

"Okay. I'll do that at the next exit," responded DC.

We exited at some small town off the I-76, stopped, and I went around to open the back. Zen promptly jumped out and dropped a "I was here" message on the nearest bush. I fiddled with his bed and arranged it so he could be comfortable. We set off and he was still unhappy.

What's the problem? *I thought.* Is he hurting? Maybe he has injured his ankle. *He had landed awkwardly when he jumped out last night. Was he hungry? He just had breakfast an hour earlier. So he shouldn't be hungry.* He is panting like he usually does when he is feeling hot.

I told DC, "Can you increase the aircon? Zen may be feeling hot at the back".

Over the increased noise of the aircon fan, I asked DC, "Do you think he ate something in the morning?"

DC: "No."

Me: "Was his stomach okay?"

DC: "Yes."

127

Me: "Was he limping?"

DC: "No. Let's give him few more minutes. He usually settles down when we are on the expressway."

A few minutes later...

Me: "He's still not comfortable. I can hear him breathing heavily. Maybe his mattress has moved again."

DC: "So, what do you want to do?"

I heard the exasperation in DC's tone. It irritated me and I snapped back. "Why do you have to discount everything I say? He's not comfortable!"

DC (in a resigned tone): "Alright. Do you want to get a new mattress?"

Me: "Yes. I am Googling the nearest pet store."

After a few minutes, we arrived at a PetSmart superstore. It was in what looked like an industrial area. Zen was happy to get out of the car and go shopping with me. We came back to the car armed with a slimmer, firmer daybed. Now to tackle the problem of how to make it more comfortable for the pup

Then I had a brainwave. "Let's cut his old mattress in half and line one side of the car with it. We'll put the other half against the duffel. He will have soft, cushiony walls on both sides and it will also block the sun coming in." DC nodded assent. Hmm...that's surprising, *I thought.* DC rarely agrees on something so quickly without adding some two bit ideas.

After twenty minutes of cutting and arranging, which Zen observed lazily, we were done. He jumped in and we set off.

Looks like AC had solved the problem. I felt comfortable. I was wrapped in a soft, cool cocoon. It was then that I realized what had been bothering me all this while. The sun muscling its way through the side quarter window was baking me. It had been fine when we were up in the mountains. It got hot and uncomfortable as we descended into the plains. The heat was overwhelming the air conditioning. Now, a piece of my mattress was blocking the sun. Over the next few minutes, the back cooled down noticeably. *Aha!* I settled down and peace returned to the car. *Yay, AC! Thank you.* We shared an unspoken spiritual bond, an extra-sensory relationship. AC could sense my feelings even when I didn't twitch a whisker, like my discomfort on the first night in their home. I could talk through my eyes, a "Zen gaze". I would use it for various purposes. For example, it could interrupt AC's slumber, like a gentle wake-up call. I would sit by the bed giving the sleeping figure the "Zen gaze." The figure would stir and the soft brown eyes would open and look at me. They would say, "Hi, doggy. Are your eyes talking to me again?" The gaze never worked on DC. I usually had to jump on that snoring figure to wake it up.

Unlike some of the featureless stretches of land in Utah, the cornfields of Nebraska were green and soothing to the eyes even though we were whizzing by at 80 miles per hour. Or so I was told. I was fast asleep most of the time after the stressful morning and the hectic three days in the Rockies. AC and DC decided on a few impromptu side trips along the I-80 while I was snoozing. Typical of them to spring a surprise, usually a pleasant one.

The first side trip was to a historic Pony Express Station in Gothenburg. The station is a simple log cabin that was built in 1854. Originally located on the Oregon Trail, southwest of Gothenburg, it was used as a fur trading post and ranch house. It functioned as a Pony Express waystation from 1860 to 1861. It was moved to its present location in 1931 and turned into a museum twenty-three years later. It has actual artifacts of that era like the list of riders who passed through and photographs. The most interesting artifact is the replica of the saddle used by the riders.

The Pony Express was a nineteenth-century startup of the Wild West, meant to disrupt the communications industry. Before the telegraph and the railroad connected the East Coast to the West Coast, messages were hand-carried across the continent—or sailed around it. The mail was loaded on a steamship from New York to Panama. Then it was taken overland by mule or train to the Pacific coast, where it was loaded on another steamship bound for San Francisco. The first overland mail service, set up in 1851 between Salt Lake City and Sacramento, took 30 days for the mail delivery, if it was ever delivered. Indian attacks and bad weather affected delivery times and risked the lives of the mail carriers. In 1860, three entrepreneurs set up a horse courier service called the Pony Express. Riders would carry documents 1,900 miles from Independence, Missouri to Sacramento, California. All for a princely sum of $5 (today's $144). They would change horses every ten to twelve miles at a waystation., like the one now in Gothenburg. The founders had to invest big bucks to set up 150+ stations, buy horses, hire riders, and pay for maintenance and upkeep. Each rider traveled about 75 miles in a day.

The Pony Express played a pivotal role in the history of the nation. In April 1861, civil war seemed imminent. California had not decided whether to support the Union or the Confederacy. Abraham Lincoln had just been elected president. His inaugural address was meant to sway the Californians in favor of the Union. Pony

Express riders carried the document from St. Joseph, Missouri to Sacramento, California in seven days and seventeen hours. A journey that usually took ten days. Bowza!!!

Unfortunately, the business model was not scalable. Revenue was weak; the expected government (snail) mail contract didn't materialize. The completion of the transcontinental telegraph sounded the death knell for the young Pony Express. It lasted only eighteen months. "Fail fast" was the mantra even in the nineteenth century. The founders lost $200,000 (almost $6 million at today's prices) and filed for bankruptcy. Bowza again!!

Pony Express riders jumped off their horses, changed saddles, and continued riding on a new horse in less than 30 seconds.

The second side trip was to Shelton. AC tried to chase down a mysterious (but supposedly Instagram famous) sculpture in a mythical pond in the town. The website labelled it as the "Bicentennial Wind Sculpture." I heard AC reading out the directions: "It is in the I-80 westbound rest area at milepost 270, two miles west of exit 272. In the pond north of the parking lot." The sculpture had garnered enough positive reviews for us to go hunting. The hunt ended at a granary. No sculpture, no pond. Sufficiently frustrated at the absence of both, we decided on the age-old method of asking the locals.

Shelton is a very small town with one main street and a few side streets. It was early evening and most of the stores on the main shopping drag were closed except for Larry's Market, the local grocery store. While DC and I waited near the checkout aisle, AC wandered up to the cashier, an old matronly lady.

"Hi. Good evening. We are looking for a wind sculpture in a pond nearby," AC said.

"A sculpture, here? There ain't no sculpture here. There's no pond either. Who told you?" responded Cashier Lady.

"We saw it on a website. Here's the photo." AC showed her the picture on the phone.

"Ha! I'm sure it is a fake. Nothing like that around here," said Cashier Lady. Turning to a young boy, she asked, "Burt, you seen any pond here?"

"Nope. No pond here," the kid replied.

In the spirit of helping strangers, Cashier Lady asked loudly, "Guys, anyone see a pond or a sculpture in a pond around here?" There were a lot of puzzled looks and one grizzled old man said, "Cathy, the only pond here is the one on my farm and it sure don't have any sculpture. I can take them to my pond and show them the fish in there." A few guffaws erupted along the line.

"Are you the ones with the California license plates?" he asked, looking pointedly at DC and me.

I heard DC mumble, "Yeah, we are."

"Then you have driven a long way for nothing," he continued with a widening grin.

We beat a hasty retreat and exited, not wishing to provide any more laughs to the locals.

The hunt had ended and we had seen nothing. AC didn't take the embarrassment very well and DC decided that it was best to keep quiet. Silence reigned in the car till we reached Omaha, when Google Map's sultry voice piped up and declared, "You have arrived."

I thought our Airbnb in Omaha was great. It was a house with a small backyard and a huge dog park, Hanscom Park, a short walk away. DC had booked it because of its proximity to the dog park. AC, though, found the neighborhood a bit rundown and unsafe and told DC grumpily, "Why don't you read the reviews properly before booking such places?"

DC didn't respond to that comment except to say, "Why are you so grumpy?" That was a dumb comment. Even I knew why AC was grumpy.

I could sense the tension between the two. *Wonder when it will blow up?* I thought.

Omaha was an important stop for the pioneers traveling westward along the Oregon and Mormon Trails. More than 600,000 passed through in twenty years in the mid-1800s. To commemorate these journeys, the city council has built a park in downtown Omaha called Pioneer Courage Park. It has a set of sculptures depicting a wagon train crossing a dry riverbed.

The sculptures memorialize the fearless spirit of the wandering pioneers, who braved death from a multitude of sources—inclement weather, native Indians bent on killing them, starvation, or just exhaustion. There are various scenes in the tableau. One is a wagon stuck in the mud. Another one is the trail boss riding his horse behind the wagons. Yet another shows women and children walking, and bison scattering away from the wagons. The artists have deliberately built the sculptures to be larger than life. Even their dogs were much larger than me. At least these sculptures were real.

.The humans in Omaha are friendly to dogs, way friendlier than anyone we had met so far in the journey. To my horror, they called me "pretty boy." *Pretty boy, really?* In the human world, "pretty" is generally associated with girls. Last I checked, my boy parts were still intact. Maybe it's one of those Americanisms, like gas instead of petrol. Even the waiter in the restaurant where we had dinner looked at me and exclaimed, "What a pretty boy! He is gorgeous. Look at those eyes." The "pretty boy" moniker I got in Omaha stuck to me for the rest of the trip. A few weeks later, I would meet a lady in a street in Vermont and she would also call me "pretty boy." She would also say that I have angel wings.

Dinner was exciting for another reason. The simmering tension between my humans finally boiled over and caused a meltdown. Throughout the day, AC had been moody and grumpy, not a very Amenable

Companion. My doggy antennae were picking up these signals since the mattress episode in the morning. The terse exchange at our Airbnb in the evening was also fraught with tension. The embarrassing search for the elusive sculpture had added to the grumpiness. We were seated on the patio of a charming Mediterranean restaurant called Della Costa in downtown Omaha. The evening was a bit warm. The patio was encircled by a metal grille. One side looked down on the street. The other side overlooked a small park. It was the perfect place for me to be off the leash but still safe. I couldn't run into traffic to say hello to another dog or rush into the park to play. I was lying down in my usual pose, chin resting sideways on my forelegs, the aroma of food in my nostrils, idly watching a poodle do her business in the park. The waiter came by and after his "pretty boy" exclamations, he turned his attention to my humans.

Waiter: "Good evening, what can I get you guys?"

AC: "Just water, please."

DC: "Can I get a Coke, please?"

Waiter: "Sure, let me get your drinks and then I can take your order."

AC: "Why do you have to drink Coke all the time?"

DC: "I like Coke with Italian food."

AC: "Have you looked at the menu? The food is not even Italian. It's Mediterranean."

DC: "Okay, so? What's your problem? I can drink Coke whenever I want."

There was a brief silence. *Uh oh!* I thought. *This is not good.*

DC: "Why are you so grumpy? You have been fighting with me since the morning."

I could hear some sniffling and my ears perked up. I sat up.

AC: "I don't like sitting in the car for so long. I don't like it when you don't listen to me. I don't like where we are staying. I didn't want to do this road trip. You always want to do things your way. Anything I say is always met with a 'NO.'"

DC (in an angry tone): "Then you should have done the bloody bookings! Wasn't the road trip your idea?"

Even more sniffling...

AC (through tears): "Yes. But I did not think I would be sitting for so many hours in a car and staying in crappy places."

DC (angrily): "You should have flown to New Jersey and Zen and I could have driven."

AC: "Yes. Maybe I will take a flight from here and YOU and YOUR dog can drive there!"

Silence.

I was standing up by now and inching closer to AC, who seemed to be more in need of some Zen love. I could smell the salt in the water on AC's face. Sadness. The same feeling I had sensed in Singapore on Mon Ami, many months ago. Instinctively I went to the aggrieved party and avoided the angry one. Safer...you never know when one can become collateral damage. I went up to AC and gave a nuzzle and a wet lick. I felt a pat on my head. The arrival of the waiter with the drinks seemed to defuse the situation. Dinner was ordered and eaten in silence. There was no conversation on the drive back to the Airbnb either, and all went to sleep without a word. There was no tension in the air when we woke up the next day. It looked like AC and DC had left last night's disagreement at the restaurant, where it rightfully belonged.

DC, always interested in World War II, was intrigued by an internet article about a Japanese balloon bomb exploding over a neighborhood in Omaha. The site is marked by an indistinguishable plaque.

In 1944, nearing the end of World War II, the Japanese tried an innovative but futile tactic to cause chaos in the US. It was codenamed Fugo. They released 6,000 bomb-carrying helium balloons from Japan with the intention of causing forest fires along the US Pacific Coast, thereby disrupting the war effort. The balloons swept across the Pacific Ocean, and landed in various sites from British Columbia to Mexico. The farthest balloon was found ten miles from Detroit. One balloon exploded over the Dundee neighborhood in Omaha, without causing any casualties. US Army censors successfully clamped down on the news about these balloons, thereby stopping any panic from occurring. Project Fugo was a failure.

AC has this thing for iconic people's homes. We had visited Steve Job's house in Palo Alto. Next was Warren Buffet's house in Omaha. I could sense AC's wishful thinking, *Maybe I can get an impromptu lunch date with him without paying for the privilege.* Every year, Buffett auctions a private lunch date for charity. People from all over the world bid thousand of dollars to get a seat at the table, hoping that some of the Buffett magic will rub off on them. Proceeds from the auction are given to the Glide Foundation, a charity Buffett supports. The highest bid has been 3.5 million dollars. Bowza!

Buffett's house was simple and modest. Suffice it to say that his wealth and influence are far bigger than his home. Sadly, I never got invited in for lunch. Maybe because DC didn't allow me to knock :-(.

CHAPTER 9

Charlie's Famous Horseshoes

"**L**et's stop for lunch at Mama Hawk's kitchen," said AC. "The Google rating is 4.8 and it's only six miles off the highway in Hamilton. Small detour." My human companions had decided to spice up their gastronomic life. "Surprise me" was the approach. From day one of our trip, all our meals were courtesy of Yelp or Google recommendations. AC had discovered that Yelp worked well for the bigger cities, while the Google ratings were more representative of the quality of food and ambience in the smaller towns. I still remember the delicious scones from Barking Dog Cafe in a tiny town called Lyons in Colorado and the oh-so-soft, melt-in-your-mouth butter buns from Wheatfields Bakery in Old Market Omaha. Yumm!

We had left Omaha early in the morning and were on our way to the historic town of Springfield, Illinois. In keeping with the spirit of the trip, DC was avoiding the expressway and driving on Route 36 through Missouri. Beautè Noire slowed and exited.

> *US Route 36 is designated by the Missouri Transportation Department as the "The Way of American Genius." Notable innovators like Samuel Clemens (Mark Twain), Walt Disney, General John "Blackjack" Pershing, and JC Penny were born or lived in towns along Route 36.*
>
> *Small towns like Chillicothe and St Joseph have produced gems of innovation, like the first automatically sliced bread and the first Pony Express ride, respectively.*

The humans' words, accompanied by the change in the speed and a different road noise, alerted me to a possible stop. We drove into the center of Hamilton and found Mama Hawk's on Davis Street. The air was hot. The tarmac was hotter. Singed my paws. *Owzaa!*

Mama Hawk's was a cozy cafe manned by two friendly young women. One of them spotted me and came out from behind the counter, uttering the dreaded words, "Oh, look at you…. Such a pretty boy!" Despite my misgivings, I gave her the Zen welcome.

The few tables inside were occupied, so we sat outside on a wooden picnic bench under a gigantic umbrella. The neighboring table was occupied by a senior relative and her two also-senior humans. The senior relative was grumpy;

she snarled at me as I trotted across to say hello. Maybe she was feeling the heat or maybe she was in a mood or maybe she was just old and grumpy. I left her alone and came back into the shade under the bench. Her two human companions were friendlier and the gentleman struck up a conversation with DC. Listening to snatches of the conversation, I figured out that they had come here from Florida. It was like an annual pilgrimage. Every summer, the three of them—gentleman, gentlelady, and grumpy dog—would drive two and a half thousand miles from Jacksonville, Florida to Omaha to visit their daughter. The stop in Hamilton was a ritual. The gentlelady was into quilting. Hamilton is the quilting capital of the US. Prior to 2008, Hamilton was a run-down town in rural northwestern Missouri. Shuttered storefronts and abandoned buildings dotted the main street. In 1995, the arrival of a housewife from California, Jenny Doan, and her start-up, Missouri Star Quilt Co., started the transformation of this town into a tourist destination. This is her story:

In 1995, Jenny and her husband were declared bankrupt. They moved to Hamilton with their three kids for a bucolic lifestyle. Her husband took up a job as a machinist in town. Jenny started sewing quilts for friends and selling them. For a decade, it remained a fulfilling but low-revenue business.

Fast forward to 2008. Realizing that demand far exceeded supply, Jenny's son and daughter bought her a quilting machine. Missouri Star Quilt Company was founded. Business was still slow. Her son realized the need to use the power of the internet to grow Jenny's business. He suggested she post some quilting tutorials on YouTube. By 2017, Jenny had become a YouTube sensation in the seemingly staid world of quilting. Her 500+ videos had garnered more than 135 million views.

Now, fans travel from all over the world to Hamilton to meet her and spend money in her stores. The gentlelady we met at Mama Hawk's is one of her fans. She is one of the more than eight thousand tourists that visit this tiny town (population 1,900) monthly. Missouri Star Quilt Co. has achieved an annual revenue of $40 million, employs more than 450 people, and has investments in four restaurants, twelve quilting supply stores, and two retreat centers. It is a rags to riches story and a lesson in how a successful business can change the fortunes of a town in rural America. Bowzaa!

Missouri Star Quilt Co. is not the only retail story in Hamilton. James Cash Penny, or JC Penny, as he is more famously known, was born near Hamilton and got his first sales job, in 1895, working in a dry goods store in town. In 1902, he launched his first Golden Rule Store. Over the next few years, the number of Golden Rule stores increased dramatically. By 1912, there were 34 stores all over the US and in 1924 he opened his 500th store in Hamilton. There must be something magical in the air.

Route 36 became I-72 as we crossed Mark Twain Memorial Bridge into Illinois on our way to Springfield. Abraham Lincoln campaigned from Springfield, Illinois to win his presidency, and so did President Obama in 2008. Everything here is Old Abe or Mr. Lincoln.

Our digs at the recently renovated Holiday Inn Express in Springfield were nice. Big modern room, great outdoor area with lots of grass and doggy missives—the last bit is interesting only for me.

A must-visit place for a foodie like DC is Charlie Parker's Diner.

AC didn't want to have dinner and the diner was not pet-friendly, so Zen kept AC company back in the hotel. I drove out to enjoy the classic American diner experience. Good old-fashioned meat, fries, and thick shakes. I was excited and salivating at the prospect of a hearty dinner. It was the first time I had the opportunity to visit an iconic diner on this trip. Charlie Parker's Diner is a Quonset hut—a prefabricated metal structure, semicircular in shape. The hut design was introduced in WW2 by the US Navy, as it was easy to assemble and ship. As a military history buff, it held a special significance for me. The owners got it cheap ($1000) and set it up on an empty plot.

I ordered their signature dish, a calorie bomb called Charlie's Famous Horseshoes. It is a big plate of a protein of your choice, in my case thick slices of ham, layered onto an English muffin and covered with French fries. Springfield is famous for its horseshoe sandwich. It was created by chef Joe Schweska in 1920. A traditional horseshoe is an open-faced sandwich that uses two slices of white toast, topped with thick slices of ham, covered with French Fries and doused with cheese sauce. I was wondering why it is called a "horseshoe." The toast and ham are shaped like a horseshoe and the fries are the nails.

As if my order was not artery clogging enough, I also ordered a vanilla Charlie's Big Shake to go with it. I sat at the table surrounded by the classic accoutrements of diner service, a fork and knife wrapped in a paper napkin, a tray of ketchup, mustard, and A1 steak sauce and a sticky pancake *syrup dispenser. The red and white checkerboard pattern of the tablecloth, the painted figures on the walls, the photos of famous personalities who had visited the diner at the entrance, the rock n' roll music playing on the radio, all evoked the Sixties. Not that I knew what the Sixties were like here, but I savored the feeling. The food arrived and the rest is history. Suffice it to say that I skipped breakfast the next morning.*

AC and DC decided to make this part of the trip into a food fest, and their version of a food fest is going to the same restaurant on two consecutive days. They did that in Omaha, visiting the Della Costa (of AC meltdown fame), and in Springfield, it was Maldaner's. The restaurant was established in 1884, way before Charlie Parker's Diner was a gleam in somebody's eye. The outdoor street seating was covered and fenced off, a common feature in the restaurants AC and DC pick, so I can chill and not be a nuisance while they eat. DC had a very satisfied look after dinner, so the food must have been good. It smelled delicious. Regrettably, AC did not oblige me this time.

The next day AC and I visited the Lincoln Home National Historic site. America loves its history and they go to extraordinary lengths to preserve it or recreate it. This museum is truly spectacular—four square blocks restored to their 1860 appearance. The houses and streets are representative of those times. As we wandered around, we could imagine Lincoln's neighbors celebrating after his presidential election win. We left Zen with a friendly ranger and took a tour of Lincoln's *house. The furniture and the decor in the house have been faithfully replicated. Though he was born dirt poor, he worked his way up in the legal profession to lead a comfortable life. He also had hired help at home (not a slave) who earned a princely sum of $1.50 a week.*

The Lincoln Presidential Museum is in a separate part of town. It is a multimedia fest of his life, from the replica of the log cabin in Kentucky where he was born to a huge diorama of the Cabinet in the White House discussing the first draft of the Emancipation Proclamation. In the log cabin diorama, Lincoln is sitting with his dog, a yellow Lab mix named Fido. When Lincoln got elected president, Fido could have been the "First Dog," but he never made it to Washington. The festivities and the furious activity following Lincoln's victory overwhelmed Fido and he became a nervous wreck. The Lincolns decided that the life in Washington would not be good for Fido and that it would be in his interest to be adopted by a family in Springfield. John Roll, one of Lincoln's oldest friends, took him in. Fido spent many good years with the Roll family till he too met with a tragic end. In an uncanny turn of events, Fido was knifed to death by a drunk on the street a year after Lincoln was assassinated. Fido was the first presidential dog to be photographed and is widely credited for the moniker "Fido," which is used as a generic term for a dog nowadays.

> *Approximately 15,000 books have been written about Lincoln, which puts him behind only Jesus Christ as the most written-about person ever!*

Zen made history too: the first non-service dog from Singapore and Palo Alto to sleep in the hallowed lobby of the Abraham Lincoln Presidential Library and Museum. It was hot outside, he was tired, and we were not done. So while AC and I took turns visiting the exhibits, he was passed out on the cool marble floor near the reception. The museum staff allowed us that luxury.

The next morning we took a side trip to the University of Illinois, Urbana-Champaign. My one-liner conclusion: Urbana-Champaign is nowhere as pretty as Stanford. You can call me snooty!

Our next destination was Gettysburg, 750 miles away, too long for a day's drive. So we halted overnight in Dublin, Ohio. This time we were in a suite at Cloverleaf, another impressive AC achievement! I was wondering why they picked Dublin. The answer revealed himself an hour later, a really close school friend of DC. He came armed with tasty Mexican food. We spent a good evening together by the poolside, or rather AC and DC did. I started by hanging around, all bright eyed and bushy tailed, hoping for some Mexican food, of which I got none, and finished by snoring away under the dining table.

Next morning, though, was superfragilisticexpiali-docious. I was prancing around in my very own private park by the Scioto river. Well...it was a park on a weekday morning. No one else was around and so it was mine, all mine until it started raining. Bowza! Trust the human gods to douse doggy happiness with a shower!

To be honest, I didn't mind the rain at all. As you read in my Lake Tahoe area adventures, splashing in all kinds of water is my constant joy. But I think DC did mind, toweling me dry is hard work. Not only am I big, but I also move around a lot. I love the rubdown, squirming, wriggling, twisting, play-biting the towel. DC usually works up a sweat.

Our next stop after Gettysburg would be in Warren, New Jersey. The first leg of our journey would be over. We would have crossed the continental United States. DC obviously loved the trip so far. AC was pleasantly surprised that it was possible to spend all that time with a significant other without acrimony. As a family, we had worked out our discordant notes and settled into a melodious happy tune. The music started in the morning, as we loaded the car and planned the route with a stop at a Yelp-rated coffee shop, the beginning gentle tones of an exciting day ahead. It rose like the recitative part of an opera toward the middle of the day with the side trip for a surprise lunch break, and ended with a flourish post dinner as we gave up our tired bodies to the sweet embrace of sleep.

CHAPTER 10

Four Score and Seven Years Ago...

The tour guide said, "The women ghosts here smell of rosewater. It was the perfume used in those days."

Do ghosts smell? I took a sniff. Then another, deeper sniff.

Nope. Nothing here!

We were on a tour of the paranormal in downtown Gettysburg. It was 8 PM and the tour guide, appropriately turned out in period costume, was regaling us with stories of amputations and survival, of bullet holes and ghosts, as we and a family of four walked with him through the streets.

We had driven through the Appalachians, rolling green hills, gentle and serene, starkly different from the craggy, striking beauty of the Sierras and the Rockies.

The two-lane highway rolled through small historical towns. I couldn't snooze much in the back because it was kinda winding, but DC enjoyed the drive along mountain roads. I was relieved when we reached the Courtyard by Marriott, Gettysburg in the early evening. This one was another AC winner. Apart from being big-dog friendly, it had a huge lobby and the hallway outside our room was the biggest I had seen so far. The length of the hallway and the thick carpet gave me the perfect excuse for Zoomie time. Bowzaa!

Gettysburg is the site of one of the most brutal and pivotal battles of the Civil War. The Union emerged victorious after three days of unforgiving conflict. Both sides together suffered more than 50,000 casualties, making it the bloodiest battle of the war. The citizens of Gettysburg (population 2,400 at that time) were left reeling in the aftermath. Any standing structure— barn, church, house—was converted to a field hospital to tend to the more than 20,000 wounded, Union or Confederate notwithstanding. An estimated six million pounds of human and animal carcasses lay strewn across the field in the summer heat. Apparently, everyone went around with a bottle of peppermint oil to counteract the smell of the carnage. This was just one battle of the war that lasted four horrific years and resulted in the largest loss of American life in history. More than 600,000 soldiers lost their lives, equivalent to 6 million in today's population.

The tour guide told us Jenny Wade's story as we walked past her house. She was the only civilian death in the three-day battle. She died in her pantry, kneading dough to make bread for the Union soldiers. During a skirmish, a bullet passed through two doors and struck her, killing her instantly. Her death was tragic, but her doomed romance with a Union soldier was even more tragic. Corporal Skelly, her fiancé, had heard of the battle in Gettysburg and had asked his childhood friend Culp, a Confederate soldier, to check on Jenny. Culp died in the battle. A few months later, Skelly also became a casualty of the war. The superstition in the Wade home is born from this tragedy. If you are single, above eighteen years of age, and you stick your ring finger through the bullet hole in the parlor door, you will get a marriage proposal within six months. I was the only bachelor in the family, and I couldn't stick my paw through the bullet hole, so AC obliged. The legend came partially true for me a few weeks later in Maine, where I met the girl of my dreams. Maybe these legends do work in the canine world as well.

We walked past the cemetery that the townspeople built to bury the dead. President Lincoln delivered his iconic Gettysburg address here in November 1863 to honor all the soldiers who died in the battle. It began with the memorable line, *"Four score and seven years ago, our fathers brought forth on this continent..."* and ended with an even more memorable line: *"the government of the people, by the people, for the people, shall not perish from this earth."*

The next day, we set out on a tour of the Gettysburg National Military Park. There are a lot of monuments honoring the sacrifices made by the brave souls in those three days. DC talked to the expert guide who joined us in the car, asking questions, listening intently.

The historical gene in me was working overtime. I had arranged for a guided tour of the battlefield at the museum. I wasn't sure if AC and Zen were as keen as I was, but they tagged along sportingly. The guide loved dogs and he was very happy to meet Zen. He was amazed that this dog had driven all the way from California. We took the conventional driving tour around the battlefield. The memorable moments were when he took us to monuments dedicated to dogs. As he said in mock seriousness, "Zen should see how dogs were involved in the war." One monument had an Irish wolfhound resting with its head on its forepaws in the classic doggy pose. The monument is dedicated to the "Fighting Irish" brigade in the army of the Potomac. The dog represents honor and fidelity. Surprisingly, the monument was sculpted by a former Confederate soldier.

Another monument was dedicated to Sallie, one of the hero dogs of the Civil War. Sallie Ann Jarrett was the mascot of the Eleventh Regiment of Pennsylvania Volunteers. She was a brindle-colored mutt with a bulldog kind of head topped with the ears of a terrier. She went to war with her regiment and had seen a lot of action. Legend has it that she could recognize all the soldiers of her regiment and greet them appropriately even when they were out of uniform. She was in the thick of the battle in Gettysburg, keeping watch over her wounded comrades for three days. Sadly, she was killed in action a month before the war ended. At the dedication of the monument in 1890, one of the veterans wrote, "The 11th Pa. has a grand monument to mark their line of battle. A bronze soldier on top, looking over the field, while the dog, Sallie, is lying at the base keeping guard." It did look like she is still looking out for them in the way her head is turned and ears are perked like she is sensing something in the far distance.

Gettysburg was bustling in the 1860s and is a thriving town today. Bars, restaurants, and shops with knick-knacks beckon the tourist dollar. In keeping with our tradition of eating at historic and unique food joints, our dinner was in Farnsworth House Inn and dessert was at Mr. G's Ice Cream on the other side of the street. Farnsworth House was built in 1810 and an adjacent brick structure was added in 1833. The house sheltered Confederate snipers, one of whom accidentally shot Jennie Wade. Bullet holes pockmark the walls of the house. Mr. G's Ice Cream is also in a house that saw action. Its south wall has bullet holes and musket ball marks as a mute testament to its role in the battle. We joined a long queue to savor their "to die for" soft serve and shakes, to quote DC. Mr. G's received our tourist dollar two days in a row. I am now familiar with the freshly made waffle cone smell. I got a teeny-weeny pup cup (I was counting my calories). Still yummy!

Ice cream did not fuel the Civil War; coffee certainly did. The plaque on a monument in Antietam dedicated to President William McKinley reads, *"Sergeant McKinley Co. E. 23rd Ohio Vol. Infantry, while in charge of the Commissary Department, on the afternoon of the day of the battle of Antietam, September 17, 1862, personally and without orders served 'hot coffee' and 'warm food' to every man in the Regiment, on this spot and in doing so had to pass under fire."*

A coffee story from DC, the coffee addict:

Coffee was an important part of the food rations during the Civil War. Soldiers drank cups of the brew at most times:

before marching, after marching, on patrol, before retiring for the night. In fact, the word "coffee" appears more often in their diaries than "rifle," "cannon," or "bullet." Generals were known to plan attacks based on when they anticipated that their troops would be the most caffeinated. The Union Army issued thirty-six pounds of coffee to each soldier annually. Men would grind the coffee themselves—some Sharps muskets came with built-in grinders in their stocks—and brew it in little brass pots called muckets. The Union Army did not have too many problems getting coffee supplies. The Confederate Army, however, suffered shortages because of the Union blockade. They had to make do with poor substitutes like roasted corn or rye or chopped beets, grinding them finely and brewing a brown and warm liquid. General George Pickett of the failed Pickett's Charge thanked his wife for such a brew, saying, "No Mocha or Java ever tasted half so good as this rye-sweet-potato blend." Arguably, coffee could be considered a weapon of war. Who would have imagined that?

This time AC decided to take a detour, to an authentically replicated Amish village in Strasburg. The Amish abhor all things tech—no Facebook or Amazon for them, no grid electricity, no phones, no cars or motorcycles. They do have propane-driven appliances like washing machines and refrigerators. Horse-drawn carriages and bicycles are their only means of transportation apart from walking. Guess who has right-of-way on the country roads?

We entered the Amish Village through the farmhouse. A barn on the side has live animals, a few chickens, a solitary cow, and a couple of horses. Another set of buildings farther down house a blacksmith and a store selling Amish-made products: handmade lace items, honey, preserves, and ice cream. Dogs are allowed on the farmhouse tour, so I went with. The familiar smell of the cow and chickens brought back puppy memories, although these smelled different from the ones in Australia. *Maybe they feed them something different here*, I thought. We wandered into the barn and with one little woof, I sent the chickens into a frenzy of clucking and squawking! How I loved it. As a pup, I would do that and the creatures would scatter, clucking in panic. Here they were in a cage, so the clucking and squawking was more intense. It also sounded different, accented.

We walked into the yard and I met what I thought was a kindred soul. Same size as me, with what looked like four ears. I went closer for a sniff and it took off, emitting a panicked "Baa" sound which elicited a surprised "WOOF" in response. Turned out to be a goat on the run! *Stupid dog! AC and DC have spent nothing on my education*, I thought.

We left behind the bucolic lifestyle of the Amish, the small country roads, and the charm of rural Pennsylvania. As late afternoon gave way to evening, we exited I-78E at Warren, New Jersey and in a few minutes parked in front of a palatial two-story home. The front door opened and Andy, AC/DC's college buddy, welcomed us with a smile. *Yay!* I thought. *This going to be good.* Back to the warmth of a family home, with bigger hugs from more humans than just AC and DC, a bedroom for more than just two nights in a row, and a HUGE park beyond the backyard fence. The neighborhood was neat and tidy, like Singapore. Perfectly manicured lawns and trimmed bushes, clean pavements and roads, and fresh green grass everywhere.

A well-deserved break after three weeks on the road and 5,300 miles from home. Even Beautè Noire heaved a sigh of relief!

PART 4B

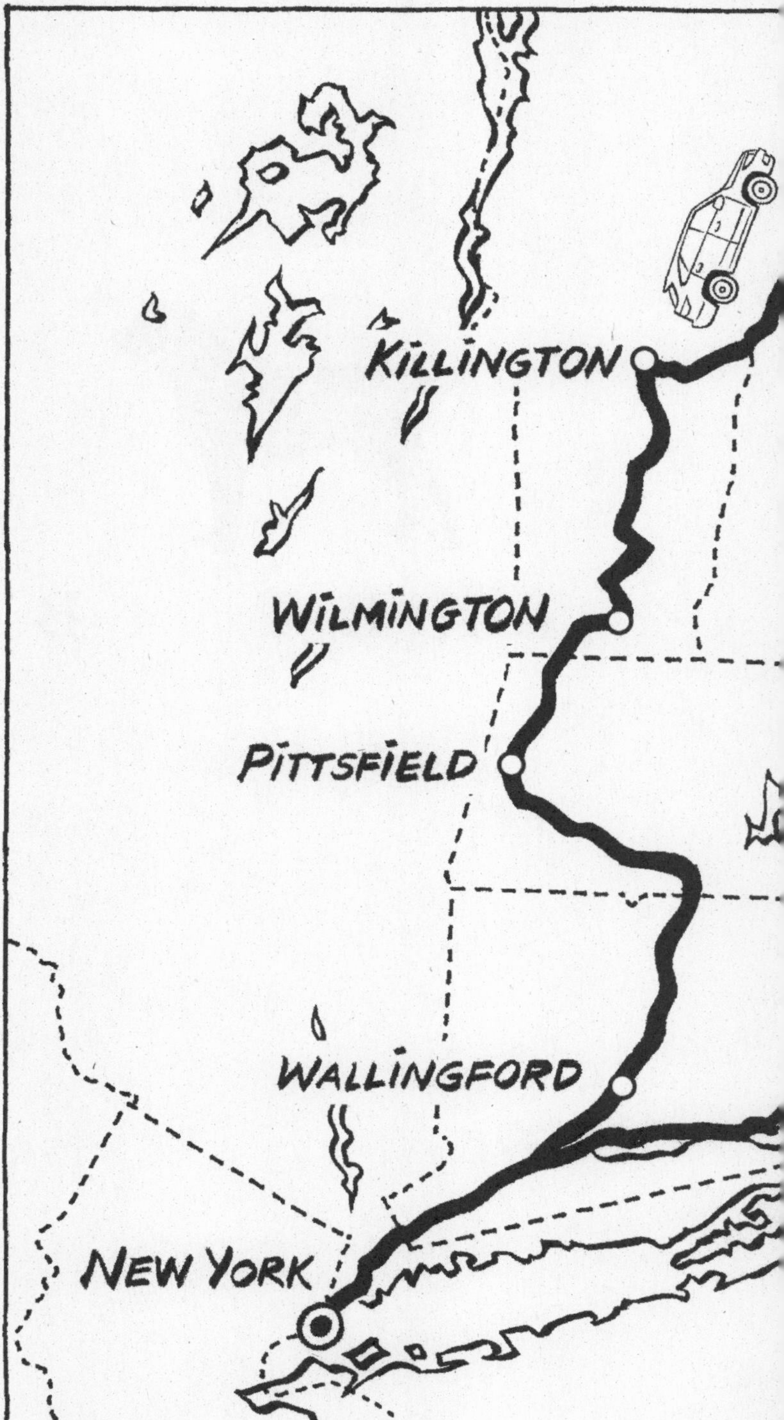
KILLINGTON
WILMINGTON
PITTSFIELD
WALLINGFORD
NEW YORK

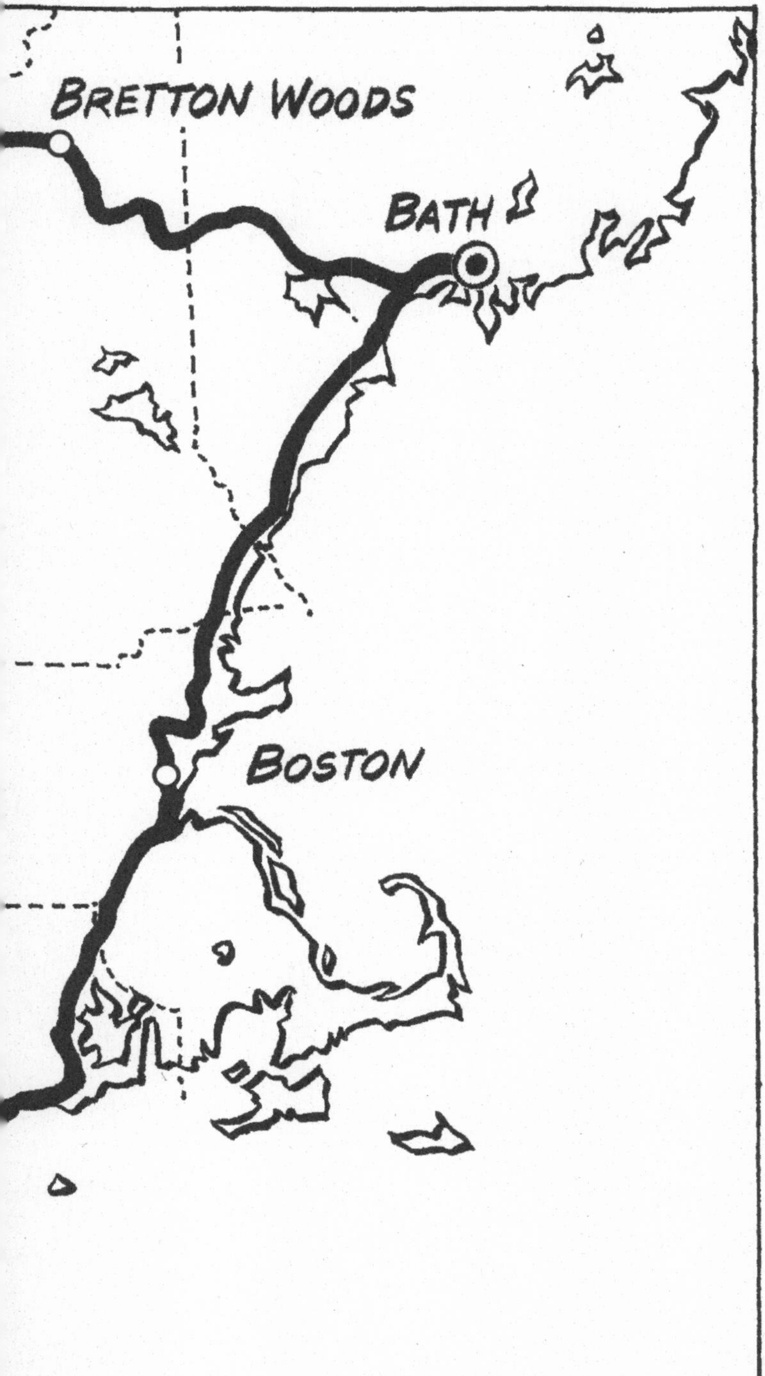
BRETTON WOODS
BATH
BOSTON

CHAPTER 11

Three Little Lies and One Big Heartbreak

"New England" is the collective name for six states in the Northeast US: Maine, Vermont, New Hampshire, Massachusetts, Connecticut, and Rhode Island. It is the oldest clearly defined region of America, with a fascinating history, that raises and answers two intriguing questions:

Firstly, why is it called "New England?"

One hypothesis is that it is based on a propaganda piece called *A Description of New England*, published in 1616 by a John Smith. He hoped to increase the number of settlers coming from England to the New World by touting the natural resources and the beauty of the region. Another hypothesis is that King James decreed that these new colonies be deemed "New England."

We will never know. The name "New England" was officially sanctioned in November 1620.

Secondly, how did the states get their names?

1. New Hampshire: This is a no-brainer. (Old) Hampshire is in England, so this one has to be "New Hampshire".

2. Vermont: French explorer Samuel De Champlain called it Verd Mont (Green Mountains). Say it fast enough and it becomes Vermont.

3. Connecticut: Derived from Quinnehtukqut (Long Tidal River), the name that Native Americans had for the Connecticut River.

4. Maine: The origins of this name are a bit sketchy. The first settlers called it "Mainland" to distinguish the area from the offshore islands. The royal court in England could never decide what to call this territory, so "Mainland" probably morphed into Maine over the years.

5. Massachusetts: Algonquins, the Native Americans who lived here, called it "Massachusèuck," which meant "about the great hill."

6. Rhode Island: Verrazano, an Italian explorer, found that the island he landed on had a striking resemblance to the Isle of Rhodes. Mapmakers subsequently referred to it as "Rhode Island."

Most of the early settlers or landowners were English, so a lot of towns have names that are identical to ones back in England: Manchester, Woodstock, Plymouth, Oxford, Bath, and so on. Warren is a very popular name. There are six Warrens in New England, one in each state. Bowzaa!

The multiplicity of names drove AC, our designated navigator, nuts. They (Google Maps and AC) had to make sure that we were going to the correct town in the right state. Imagine putting Warren, New Jersey as your destination when you want to go to Warren, New Hampshire. You would be driving in the wrong direction for a very long time.

Apart from its historical significance, New England has one of the most enchanting landscapes that we had driven through so far. Civilization and nature do a delicate dance here. Houses merge into forests and small towns emerge from the landscape. The people, the flowers, the fauna, the trees, the mountains, and the valleys are in perfect harmony. This was summer, of course, the time that life blooms and blossoms in New England. During winter it is one of the most inhospitable places on the East Coast.

Our plan was to do a leisurely eight-day drive starting from New Jersey, hugging the coast till Maine. Then we would strike out westward into New Hampshire and Vermont, turn south through Massachusetts and Connecticut, and finish in New York. A loop of about

900 miles. New England is not very big. Typically, 900 miles would have been a two or three-day drive for us, but you can't experience the beauty of this region scorching through it at 90 mph.

We left New Jersey in a huge downpour with Andy's warning, "Don't get on Tappan Zee Bridge because it will be jammed" ringing in my ears. Despite three GPSs going with alternate routings and much-heated discussions between AC and DC in the front seats, one unfortunate right turn and there we were we. Tappan Zee Bridge! Ha! My golden-brown nose would have been a better GPS. The good news was, the bridge wasn't crowded and we managed to cross it relatively quickly.

It was a very wet drive. The rain drizzled in some places and pelted down on the windscreen in others. The expressways here were quintessential New England: small lanes, gentle slopes, tarmac framed by beautiful trees that somehow seemed well manicured, and small rest stops. Interestingly, the rest stops here were different from the ones we stopped at in the Midwest. Those rest stops were huge open structures with toilets and drink-dispensing machines. The pet areas were unsheltered and often baking in the sun. New England rest stops were compact and green with coffee and fast food outlets and a gas station. The pet areas were more interesting—cool grass wet with rain, and "I was here" messages from my kind. As Beautè Noire's tailgate opened, I would stand up and sniff. DC would walk out with nose in the air, sniffing the aroma of fresh coffee.

The rain and the reduced visibility almost cost us our lives. DC was cruising at a much lower speed than normal. I could tell by the noise of the wind rushing past the windows, the sound of the tires on the road, the note of the engine—signals that my ears picked up and my brain interpreted. DC and AC were quietly chatting about something. Then I heard AC yell, "WATCH IT!"

The car swung violently to the right. I was thrown against the cushioned duffel bag and I yelped in surprise.

I heard the "Watch it!" and the "Yulp!" almost at the same instant, but I had no time to react to those sounds. I was struggling to keep the car under control.

We had been driving in the left lane of a two-lane divided expressway. It was raining heavily and the wipers struggled to keep the windscreen clear. Visibility was low. AC had been saying something to me, I don't remember what... I was listening distractedly.

A big pick-up thundered past on my right. It was a modified truck, with raised suspensions, shod with massive off-road tires. He must have been doing at least a 100 mph. Guy is crazy, I thought. In this rain, he is going to kill someone. A few seconds later, the pick-up swerved violently to the left, then veered to the right as the driver struggled to gain control. I saw one tire come off and career into our lane, bouncing joyously at its liberation.

AC yelled, "WATCH IT!" Reflexively, I turned the wheel right to avoid the tire and instinctively stabbed the brake, a huge mistake. We skidded, then fishtailed as I swung the wheel back, foot still on the brake. Like a slow motion video, the scenery in the windscreen changed from the road to trees, then back to the road, accompanied by the muted screech of rubber on the wet tarmac. I heard a thud and yelp from the back. The tire sideswiped a car in front and kept going to the right as if searching for its truck.

Out of the corner of my eye, I noticed the pick-up, on three wheels, side-swipe an MPV and send it off the road down the embankment. The bouncing tire jumped the guard rail on the right and disappeared from sight into the farmland. The pickup came to rest facing us. The driver emerged from the cab and stood looking dazed, bent over, hands on knees, shaking his head. We had come to a stop in a muddy area on the left. Another car pulled over behind the accident and stopped with hazard lights flashing. We could see passengers emerging from the MPV. AC looked at the back and, not seeing Zen, ran around the car and opened the tailgate. I stepped out and splashed my way through some puddles and joined them at the back. The pup was crouched in his corner, looking rather sorry. We got a little tail wag, the kind he would give us when he wasn't sure about something. I ran my hands over his body to check for injuries. He didn't seem to have any. Thank God for all the padding, *I thought.*

Another car stopped behind us and a young man got out and ran over. "Are you guys okay?" He saw Zen. "Is the dog okay?" he asked.

"Yes," I said, "we are all good."

When we began the trip, I had asked God for one wish, "Keep all of us healthy and safe throughout the trip." This time he granted my wish. Two years later, he wouldn't.

After this heart-stopping adventure, we resumed our drive to our destination for the day, which was Tish's home. She was in the same program at Stanford as AC and DC, and she lived in Westborough, an hour's drive west of Boston. It was still raining hard as we stopped at a large gate. DC talked into a box and magically the gate opened. We drove up a circular driveway and parked. Tish's home looked like one of the royal palaces in the English countryside, like a modern version of the castle from *Downton Abbey,* a show AC and I would watch on Netflix. At least, AC would watch and I would get this endless gentle massage.

AC and DC have gone completely crazy. Have they really have landed a room here? I thought. This was better than the Omni resort in Interlocken (which, by the way, had been my best accommodation so far). It looked plush and imposing. *Mrs. T lives the high life.* We parked in a barn-size garage next to a Rolls-Royce Phantom. The other occupants of the garage were a yellow Ferrari and an Audi R8. Beautè Noire looked completely out of place, but didn't seem to mind the company. I could imagine the conversation later:

Ferrari: "Mamma Mia, look what the cat dragged in!"

Rolls-Royce (in a clipped British accent): "By golly, what on earth is this monstrosity?"

Audi R8 (in the guttural German accent): "Das ist ein Acura, dummkopf."

Beautè Noire: "Dude, I've schlepped all the way from California; I'm wet and cold and grimy and I almost killed my family today. Fucking rain in your backyard never stops. Lose the attitude, arseholes. I'm so not in the mood."

I walked in through the door and met our host. She is a New Englander, born and brought up in Boston, very cultured and soft-spoken—like Puck's human grandpa. (Remember my twin Puck from Winslow, Arizona?) She and her husband own a very successful software services company. And she absolutely adores dogs.

"Oh my God! You are so cute," she said as I waltzed around her, huffing and chuffing in happiness. Dogs can sense if a human tolerates dogs or absolutely loves them. Her voice, her facial expression, her touch, the look in her eyes, told me that she was clearly in the "absolutely love dogs" category.

She turned to AC and said, "Thank you for accepting my invitation to stay here. Zen is so adorable." Sometime later in the night, I overheard AC telling DC, "We were invited only because of Zen."

The mansion totally rocked! I bounced off the walls (and staircases) in sheer enjoyment. Her hallway was as long as our entire block in Palo Alto and it was carpeted. I was beside myself with joy—racing in one direction, turning on a dime at the end of the hallway, and rocketing back the other way. Bowza!

I exhausted myself running around the house, up the stairs, down the stairs, out to the garden, onto the putting green, down into the basement…. Whew! I love big homes with carpets. I can race around without skidding and sliding. Sigh! I want to be adopted by Tish (I think even AC and DC may want to get adopted by her).

Like our home in Singapore, the mansion also had signs of a dog not long gone. I could still smell him everywhere. Charlie was his name. When he passed, he took a piece of Tish's heart with him. Her love for him was obvious in all the personalized items all over the house. The carpet had been laid for him to run around without skittering on the marble; he had cushions, beds, bowls in every room. He had the most awesome wardrobe—multiple leashes, collars, harnesses. She couldn't get herself to throw anything away. Tears glistened in her eyes when she talked about him: how he was too scared to visit the vet so she convinced the vet to come to the house; how she got him all those vitamins and glucosamine to strengthen his joints; how he loved to sit in the hall observing all the goings and comings of his humans. He was the royal dog and I could imagine him lording over this family.

If someone were to calculate brainpower per square mile, Boston would be in the top three cities in the US. It had the first public schooling system in America. Today, there are over a hundred different colleges and universities in Boston—Harvard, MIT, and Tufts being among the more prominent ones. It is also home to the Boston Red Sox, the legendary baseball team, and the New England Patriots, their super-achiever football team. Bostonians believe they are second to none. Even the waterfowl here had an attitude. I gave a flock of 'em the good ole Zen charge. Unlike their West Coast brethren, these guys didn't flinch. Instead I was the unfortunate recipient of withering and stern professorial glares. Retreat was the only option. DC couldn't stop laughing. Smartass!

During the colonial days, Boston was the hotbed of radical and revolutionary thought that finally culminated in the American Revolution. We got these nuggets of information from our guide during the Freedom Trail Walking Tour. The tour began from Boston Commons, apparently the oldest commons in America. Cow-grazing fields in those days were called "commons." I couldn't smell any bullshit.

We wound our way slowly to the site of the Boston Massacre. The tour guide was giving the humans a background to the massacre and I was keeping an ear out. My nose did the more important activity of savoring the bouquet in the square where we were all gathered. As I understood it, the British had beaten the French in North America and India to gain total control of those colonies. Unfortunately, they were much the poorer for it. Great Britain's debt in 1764 was 130 million pounds, equivalent to 24 billion dollars today. King George III, the monarch of Britain, and his council needed money. They turned to the age-old mechanism of getting money—raising taxes. Over the next few years, the British taxed the colonies for all sorts of items, most famously sugar, molasses, and tea. They set up tax collection mechanisms and a judiciary distinct from the colonial justice system to impose punitive penalties and punishments for non-payment.

Why did this sound so familiar?

Aha. I know. I heard DC and bro talking about it one day at Philz Cafe in Palo Alto. I distinctly remember DC saying "Did you know that RICH was an acronym during the British Raj (as the Indians refer to the British colonial period)? It stood for Rob **India** and Come Home."

Back to the tour guide's story. In New England, the locals, who thought of themselves as English, were now treated like second class citizens. Fearing that they would take up arms, Britain sent more soldiers to Boston, increasing the already simmering unhappiness. By 1770, there were 2,000 soldiers occupying a city of 16,000 colonists to enforce tax collection. There were regular skirmishes between patriot colonists and soldiers and loyalists (colonists supporting the British).

On the icy evening of March 5, this pot of simmering tension boiled over. Around 8 pm, an altercation started between a British officer and a barber's apprentice. The apprentice went away and told a few townspeople of the assault. Soon there was a small crowd of people yelling insults and tossing twigs and other sundry objects at the soldiers. About 9:15 pm, a restless mob had gathered at the Custom House, where the tax collections were stored. There was a lone soldier on guard. Someone in the crowd misidentified the soldier as the one who had assaulted the barber's apprentice. Soon the mob was baying, "Kill him. Knock him down!" The terrified soldier backed away and asked for help. The senior officer on duty, Captain Preston, arrived on the scene with seven other soldiers and took up defensive positions. Members of the incensed mob were now attacking the soldiers with clubs and sticks. Then someone said the words, "Damn you, fire." The resultant volley of bullets killed five people and blasted its way into the history books. Captain Preston had not issued the order to fire. A soldier had uttered those words. He had been knocked down with a club and had reacted in anger.

Three weeks after the massacre, Paul Revere, a hero of the American Revolution, produced an engraving entitled "The Bloody Massacre in King Street." It is probably the most effective piece of propaganda in American history.

The engraving has a dog in the middle of the melee, looking at the viewer, unconcerned by the mayhem— a symbol of loyalty and fidelity.

Whether in Springfield or Gettysburg, Boston or Lexington, Americans have taken great efforts to preserve their history, ensuring it passes down from generation to generation to instill a sense of patriotism, belonging, and pride. Ancient civilizations like India and Egypt struggle to preserve their history and fail to inculcate a sense of ownership for the country (sad face emoticon). I could see this thought bubble above DC's head.

We visited the hallowed grounds of Harvard. The university area is much smaller at 200 acres compared to Stanford's 8000 acres. This small size does not make it humble The place got attitude, bro! Then, of course, everyone and everything here had an attitude. By the end of this journey, so would I.

I would be, so far as I know, the only dog to have visited Berkeley, Stanford, Harvard, the University of Illinois, Urbana Champaign and the University of Michigan, Ann Arbor. How's that for attitude?

Every tourist who visits Harvard and every student there goes to see the statue of Mr. John Harvard. It is nicknamed as the Statue of Three Lies, referring to the inaccuracies in the inscription, which reads, "John Harvard, Founder, 1638."

Lie #1. The statue is not of John Harvard. Nobody knows what John Harvard looked like. The model used by the sculptor was Sherman Hoar.

Lie #2. He was not the founder of the university, but the first major benefactor. Harvard was officially founded by a vote by the Great and General Court of the Massachusetts Bay Colony.

Lie #3. The university was founded in 1636, not in 1638.

What's life without a little enduring controversy?

Travel west and then east to travel slightly north. We left Boston on a sunny morning and headed to Brunswick, Maine. Brunswick is 137 miles "slightly north" from Boston. I am now repeating what Google Maps tells my companions in her sultry voice: "Bear slightly right on I-90." When we reached Brunswick, the trip log reflected 239 miles. How did we manage to add 102 miles?

Well, we first went east to Lexington, the site of the first battle of the Revolution; then northwest to Salem, where they supposedly burned witches at the stake; and then northeast along the supposedly scenic Highway 1. DC soon realized that not all Highway 1s are scenic. This one was a country road, single lane, cutting through forests and small towns, nothing spectacular. It went tantalizingly close to the ocean but never close enough. I could smell the ocean but could not see it. After Salem, we meandered to Manchester-by-the-Sea before arriving at our final destination, Brunswick.

In Salem, "witches" were executed in a period of mass hysteria in the seventeenth century. The town is small. You come off the highway onto Main Street and before you know it, you are in the town center. The day we were there was the weekly holiday, and only one museum was open.

The popular idea that "witches were burnt at the stake in Salem" is completely false. Nineteen people were found guilty of witchcraft and were executed by hanging in accordance with British law. In fact, some of the witches were not women. Giles Corey was one of them. Eighty-one years old at the time of his death, he was a prosperous farmer living in Salem. He was accused of being a witch but refused to say a word at his trial. In order to extract a confession, he was sentenced to a method of torture in which heavy stones are placed on the chest of the accused till they plead guilty or die. Corey Giles died after three days.

We drove to the very pretty Manchester-by-the-Sea. The movie of the same name, shot in this town, was nominated for Best Picture and lots of other awards. Casey Affleck won Best Actor for it. I had my first-ever al-fresco dinner at a park adjoining the marina, which is in the movie too. Sitting by the water, watching boats rock gently in the breeze, inhaling the fishy aroma and a dash of celebrity will even make boring commercial dog food transform into a delicious meal. AC was getting me used to dinner with an ambience.

Our hotel in Brunswick, The Daniel, is in a historic building dating back to 1819. A very friendly receptionist greeted us, or rather greeted me, effusively and checked us in. Our room was large and comfortable, belying its age. I inadvertently contributed to the entertainment on our floor. The day had been boring, apart from the trip to Lexington. My pent-up energy needed an outlet. I have a monkey toy which starts singing in a funny tone when I squeeze it. When my monkey toy was unpacked, I grabbed it and charged out from the room into the long corridor outside. AC and DC stood at the door and watched me tear up and down with this singing thingy in my mouth. I must have been on my second round when the door to the adjacent room opened and an elderly gentleman peeped out to check the source of the commotion. He saw me running around and smiled. I was in the midst of a Zen Zoomie. Soon another door opened and a kid looked out. "Hey, Mom. You have to come and see this." Being the consummate entertainer, I gave the audience a few more laps, then retreated to our room with cheers following my departure from the stage.

We visited Bath, the "City of Ships"—the shipbuilding hub in the late nineteenth and early twentieth centuries. Bath even today builds destroyers for the US Navy. While we were there, DC whispered quietly in my ear, "It's AC's birthday today, so let's behave. And we need to clean you up. A bath in Bath is in order" (smiling at the joke). I hadn't had a bath for more than a month and probably smelled to high heaven from my doggy play dates all over the country. We carried baby wipes, the panacea for everything dirty: baby's bottom, dirty paws, ketchup-stained fingers, you get the picture. AC had been wiping me down with those awfully scented wet wipes for a while. Still, it was no substitute for a real bath, which I got today. They bathed me at Wags & Whiskers, a pet store in historic downtown Bath. I was good and ready for the birthday celebrations.

Pemaquid Point Lighthouse is almost 200 years old. It was commissioned in 1827 by John Quincy Adams. Its light is visible 14 miles out.

The image of the lighthouse is on the state quarter and it is also a background for Windows 7.

A friendly old lady in the visitor center told us about a great massage place and a must-see lighthouse. AC promptly signed up for the massage and left DC and me to our own devices. We strolled past some historic shops, looking for the local cafe. We found one and DC used this opportunity to do some research on the best place to stop for birthday lunch. AC is not a birthday dinner person. We picked a well-known restaurant (according to our trusted reviewer, Yelp) called The Schooner's Landing in the little town of Damariscotta. It was meant to be a surprise for AC, who was told that we were headed to Pemaquid Lighthouse. In the back of the car, I was unusually restless, excited to celebrate the birthday—and I love surprises.

We drove into Damariscotta and parked outside the restaurant. The Schooner's Landing is very popular, as evidenced by the number of cars in the lot. The outdoor dining area is set on the boardwalk under a giant tent roof.

DC said, "Let's grab lunch." I hopped out and smelled oyster, fish and chips, and a whole lot of French fries. DC whispered something to the hostess and she gave us a table on the edge, overlooking the water. I could see waves lapping through the gaps in the boardwalk. A cheerful waitress took our order and DC whispered something into her ear. I briefly caught the words "birthday cake." Our meal—sorry, their meal—arrived and it was one of the best meals that I sniffed at in this entire trip... but only sniffed at, because I did not get my degustation menu from AC. After the main course, AC's birthday cheesecake arrived, with our cheerful waitress and her colleague singing "Happy Birthday to You."

I accompanied the song with my "kangaroo hop." AC believes that I learned it in my birth country, Australia. It's one of those moves where I hop on my hind legs with tail wagging wildly. Apparently it is a very cute routine. I got a big hug and a kiss from AC for my performance (thank God for the bath), but only a perfunctory lick of the birthday cheesecake.

Pemaquid Point will remain etched in my memory for a very long time. It was where I met my first true love.

I have an infatuation with Agatha at my sitter's home in Santa Clara. I treat Aish's house as my second home. I was very comfortable with her from the first day we met. There was a calming, loving presence about Aish that I loved. Agatha was the other dog she looked after during the day. She and I would have a rollicking time in the garden. Yet my feelings for her were nothing compared to those about to be awakened.

AC and I were wandering on the lawn outside the lighthouse when I met Lynda from Ohio, with her grandfatherly human companion. Unlike Gracie, who I had met on the forty-niners' trip and who was fun but could be only a buddy, Lynda evoked something deeper in me. Her pheromones triggered an instant love. I wanted her in a different way. As we circled each other, sniffing and licking, I knew she was the one. Unlike a human, I can make up my mind pretty quickly. She was going to be my mate.

We promptly started playing. I was at my gentlemanly best and allowed her to jump all over me. She would barrel into me, I would take the hit and roll over, then we would wrestle each other.... She would suddenly stop, stand up, and look the other way...acting disinterested. I would lick her ear furiously and BAM—she would turn around and hit me again. We were both on our leashes and that made the play a little more restrictive than I had planned, but I wasn't complaining. The tangled leashes brought us closer together. The touch of her flanks and her soft bites sent me into raptures. She was playful, naughty, gentle. I was so falling for her. Her musk was raging through my nasal passages and triggering unknown sensations in me.

After another bout of maniacal play, I had enough and spread myself out on the grass, panting from my exertions. She flopped down next to me. The cool sea breeze, the warmth of the sun, the rise and fall of her side against mine…life couldn't have been better. Then I heard Grandpa say, "Oh, there they are." I turned around to see a young couple and a small kid coming from the lighthouse. He continued, "That's my son and his family. They are spending summer with us."

The little girl was bouncing over to us like all little kids do, hopping on one foot and trotting on the other one. "Lynda…Lynda…" she was screaming at the top of her voice. "Look, Mom, there they are," she said, pointing to us. Lynda sprang up at the sound of her name and gave her little human a body wag.

The older humans walked over and the man said, "Hi, Dad, who is this?"

Grandpa said, "This is Zen."

"Hi, Zen." He bent over to say hello. I had sensed their arrival meant that my time with Lynda was limited and her departure was imminent. I promptly gave him my best body wag in the hope that they would stand around and chat a bit longer. Lynda had left my side and was playing with her little human. *That's not right. She is supposed to play with me,* I thought as I went over to them, dragging AC along. Lynda turned to me and gave my ear a wet lick. It felt good.

Then the man said, "We've got to go, Dad."

Grandpa turned to AC and said, "It was nice meeting you. Have fun for the rest of the day."

"Come on, Lynda, let's go. See you, Zen." He patted me on the head.

And just like that, the time for our separation had come. My doggy intuition was right. They were going to leave. The canine gods were not going to help my budding romance. The pat on the head felt like someone had taken a hammer to my skull. I stood there, stunned... disappointed...hurt...unhappy. The sun suddenly felt hot and the sea breeze went missing. The universe had conspired against me. I could see Lynda straining against her leash, looking back at me, wanting to come back to me, be my companion. Grandpa handed the leash over to the man, who said curtly, "Lynda, let's go." She stopped straining at her leash and walked away from me, out of my life.

"Bye, Lynda," I heard AC say. That's the last I saw of her. Our blossoming romance on the shores of Maine was not to be, and my heart broke into a million pieces.

Sitting in the back of the car, tired and morose, I scarcely noticed that we shot past our hotel and took a detour to Freeport, an outlet shopping destination site in Maine and home to one of America's oldest brands, the venerable L.L. Bean. It sells everything from clothes to kayaks, and in Freeport the L.L. Bean has a restaurant as well. Their stores, which occupy a large section of main street in downtown Freeport, are very dog friendly; they have doggy water bowls inside on every floor and an entire doggy section. We sat down for dinner at a tavern across their flagship store. The food was not so great— AC gave them a 1 star rating. I also gave AC and DC a 0.5 star for dinner that evening. They served me dinner in L.L. Bean's parking lot! And like an hour late! And only the entrée...no appetizer. Sometimes they treat me like a dog!!!

CHAPTER 12

Angel Wings

A handwritten puzzle on a display board caught our attention. It was set outside the Village Roost, a café in Wilmington, Vermont. *"What has four letters, never has five letters, and sometimes has six letters? Stumped? Order a coffee inside and get the answer."* The answer was also handwritten on a little board next to the barista's machine. It read:

> *The answer is in the sentence itself.*
> *Read it like a statement and not a puzzle.... Got it?*
> *"What" has 4 letters. W, H, A, T.*
> *"Never" has 5 letters, and*
> *"Sometimes" has 9 letters.*

With our thirst for the answer sated, we settled into huge leather armchairs for brekkie (Aussie word for breakfast). The coffee, the croissants, and ambience made this a memorable one. It helped that they allowed pets inside. AC slipped me half a croissant.

We had reached Wilmington the previous evening, after a gorgeous drive from Brunswick. It had been a typical New England summer day: bright, cheerful and warm. My mood had distinctly improved by then. Lynda was a fond but distant memory. It's good that dogs live mostly in the present. Whatever happened in the past stays there. Emotional baggage and sad memories are in the human domain.

We had stopped at the Omni Mount Washington Hotel in Bretton Woods for lunch. The hotel has a very interesting history. Millionaire Charles Stickney bought the Mount Pleasant Hotel, a much smaller property, in 1881. In those days, it was an exclusive retreat in the White Mountains for the wealthy folks coming in from New York and surrounding areas by train. Stickney had ambitions of building the grandest of grand hotels. He brought in 250 Italian stonemasons and hired famous architect Charles Alling Gifford to build a magnificent state-of-the-art property. In two years, they had constructed a Renaissance Revival estate beyond compare. Each room had hot and cold running water, unheard-of fire suppressive techniques, hand plasterwork, Tiffany glass windows, and full electricity. The hotel was opened in 1902 and Thomas Edison—yes, Thomas Edison—turned the lights on for the first time at the opening ceremony. Total cost for building: 1.7 million dollars ($49 million today). It still runs its own telephone exchange and has its own post office.

The hotel entered the history books on account of the Bretton Woods Conference, held there in 1944. Nearing the end of World War II, 730 delegates from 44 Allied nations met in June 1944 to regulate the international monetary and financial system. The World Bank and the International Monetary Fund were created at this time, and so was the reserve currency system. In this system, one of the world currencies is identified as the reserve currency, in this case, the US dollar, and the reserve currency is pegged to gold. Then all other currencies are pegged to the reserve currency. Essentially this monetary system propelled the US to its superpower status today—before it collapsed in the 1970s.

The other details are too complex for my canine mind. I have a more simple system to build reserves: tail wags+ body wags + soft eyes = cuddles + "pretty boy." By the way, that adulatory term has still not gone away. Drat! Anyway, I built up a hefty reserve of cuddle holdings in a couple of hours, thanks to the hotel staff and guests.

Route 100 in Vermont is one of the top ten scenic byways in America. The 146-mile route runs along the eastern edge of the Green Mountain range and is bracketed by Waitsfield in the north and Wilmington in the South. The road plays peekaboo with the White River as it dives into valleys and rushes up hills through a tapestry of green forest. The serrated peaks of the mountain range on one side offer a stark contrast to the smooth meadows and farms on the other. During winter it is also referred to as "The Skiers' Highway." There are multiple ski resorts along its western edge.

I heard DC say, "Doesn't this remind you of the Yorkshire scenery described by James Herriot in his books?" James Herriot is DC's favorite author. He wrote a series of bestselling books on his life as a vet in Yorkshire.

James Herriot's words were playing in my mind as we cruised through Vermont.

"In the summer dusk, a wild panorama of tumbling fells and peaks rolled away and lost itself in the crimson and gold ribbons of the western sky. To the east, a black mountain overhung us, menacing in its naked bulk."

The landscape resembles an English countryside except that everything is American size—large. What would have been quaint cottages nestling together in Londonderry-Yorkshire Dales, Old England, transform to big-ass homes on three-acre plots in Londonderry-Vermont, New England. As we drove through the hills, valleys, and forests, there were no visible signs of human inhabitation till you notice the mailbox by the roadside and a little dirt road running up to a house partially visible in the trees.... Aha! There it is! The big-ass house.

You know there's a town around the corner when you see signs asking you to reduce speed to 25 mph...and voila! Main Street appears. The downtown area in most small towns in Vermont is lined with antique stores and art galleries. New England probably has the highest number of art and antique stores per capita in the US. John Steinbeck also made a similar observation in his book, Travels with Charley: "I can never get used to the thousands of antique shops along the roads, all bulging with authentic and attested trash from an earlier time. There are enough antiques for sale along the roads of New England alone to furnish the houses of a population of fifty million."

We spent some time in a charming little town called Woodstock. It seemed to be stuck in a time warp. Established in 1761, Woodstock has a population of only 3,000. A river bubbles its way through town. A few old covered bridges cross it at regular intervals. AC remarked that they looked like the ones in the famous Hollywood movie, The Bridges of Madison County. *In a throwback to the last century, all the events and other important information are written on a small blackboard in the middle of the town. Very quaint indeed. AC, Zen, and I spent a lot of time meandering through the town and soaking in the atmosphere. So serene and calm. People seemed to be walking more leisurely than they did back home. Life was really slow and I was enjoying it. AC was getting a bit antsy and wanted to move on.*

I had a scenic lunch on the balcony of The Woodstock Inn and Resort, a historic hotel set up by Laurence Rockefeller, son of John Rockefeller. I was served water in a huge ceramic bowl. Bowza! I think it tasted better.

One of the attractions put up visibly on the blackboard was a visit to a Vermont farm. After my experience with goats in Amish land, AC and DC were not sure how this visit would turn out, but they tried it. This one also did not turn out to be pretty. The smelly four-legged ones sent me into a barking, growling frenzy. I could hear Cathy's warning playing in my head, "Simba, be careful. Those cows can be nasty." I am sure my humans must have been wondering if I was born on a real farm in Australia. I did chase chickens there and the odd cow, but that was the extent of my farm upbringing.

Later that evening, we experienced the future of small hotels at The Vermont House, a Hermitage Club property in Wilmington. No human beings, no staff at reception, no concierge; just two codes sent via email to AC. One was to open the front door and the second one unlocked a box inside that contained the room keycard. And bingo, we were checked in. Even the coffee machine looked high tech.

We unloaded all our gear, freshened up (in my case, this meant swapping my harness for a red collar), and stepped out onto Main Street, looking for a nice place for dinner. It was still early evening, around 7 PM, and the summer sun had not yet set. A lady stopped in front of me and said, "Oh gosh, what a beautiful puppy." *Beats "pretty boy" anytime*, I thought. She was exuding the "I am a dog lover" vibe from every pore in her body. I gave her the best possible Zen welcome. You know, the big smile, wiggling hips, and madly wagging tail one. She squatted down and grabbed my face in her hands, gave me a chin rub and a very vigorous rub-down of my flanks. Her pants smelled of more than one dog. She offered me her chin for a "kiss" and I promptly obliged, evoking a, "Oh, you are such a darling."

She looked at AC and said, "Is he an English Lab?"

"Not really. He is from Australia, but he is English stock," AC responded.

"Interesting. He is a big boy. Look at that head…and those eyes…I haven't seen this color in a while. They are just gorgeous." AC and I were reveling in the attention being lavished on me. "Look, he also has angel wings," she continued.

"Angel wings?" AC asked in a puzzled tone, looking down at my shoulder to where the lady was pointing.

"Yes. These white markings running down his shoulders are called angel wings. At least, that's what we call them. I am a breeder and these markings are unusual. Not many dogs have such a perfect set." She ran her hands down my shoulders to show AC the markings.

"Oh yeah. They do look like angel wings," AC remarked.

So now, I am a pretty boy with angel wings. Sigh!

The tail end of our magical journey through New England was not as scenic as Maine or Vermont, but definitely more cultural and artistic.

We were driving through the Berkshires, Massachusetts—a region located at the southern end of the Green Mountains with an easygoing artsy vibe. It has famous museums like The Clark and Norman Rockwell, farm-to-table restaurants, and cafes with attitude run by tattooed young ladies. It also has one solitary peak, Mount Greylock. From the top, one can see five states. While my humans were enjoying the view, a well-fed bro and his sleek buddy walked past us. I promptly mixed it up with them. The bro had hiked up the mountain and was in no mood, but the buddy obliged. We romped around each other as far as my leash would allow. They were off-leash. Obviously their humans trusted them more than my companions.

Sir Francis Bernard, the Royal Governor from 1760–1769, gave the region its name of "Berkshire" to honor his home county in England.

I love art. DC prefers military museums. It had been a bone of contention in all our holidays till we came to an agreement. I would go to see all the art museums while DC would visit the military history museums or hunt down boutique coffee shops. I had planned to visit The Clark and the Norman Rockwell Museum, while DC and Zen could do whatever they wanted.

The Clark Art Institute in Williamstown has a phenomenal art collection and a very interesting history. It was set up by Sterling Clark, the grandson of the founder of Singer Sewing Machines, and his French wife, Francine. She had a nose for art and he had the money. Together, they amassed an extensive collection that was at first kept in their home in New York. It was moved to Williamstown in the Berkshires because of Mr. Clark's paranoia. During the Cold War, he correctly or incorrectly assumed that the Russians were more likely to bomb New York than upcountry rural areas. So, Williamstown gained a museum and New York lost one.

A few miles away from The Clark is the Norman Rockwell museum in Stockbridge. I was super excited to see Rockwell's "Triple Self-Portrait," an oil on canvas painting done in 1960. The painting shows him seated on a stool, looking at himself in a mirror and sketching in charcoal. True to his self-deprecating nature, the reflection is of a cartoonish-looking man with round eyeglasses, the antithesis of his real self. In reality, he was quite a handsome man. We also saw Norman Rockwell's work exhibited in the Ford Museum in Dearborn a week later. In 1953, Henry Ford II commissioned a calendar from Rockwell to commemorate Ford's 50th anniversary. Rockwell created a series of eight paintings, four showing Henry Ford's past and his impact on the world, and the remaining four depicting Ford Motor Company's present and future.

While in the Berkshires, I enjoyed another scenic dinner (AC was getting good at picking scenic dinner spots) by a lake on the outskirts of Pittsfield, MA. I was losing count. The view was great. The grass, however, was littered with waterfowl droppings.

The Hancock Shaker Village is near Pittsfield. The Shakers are a farming community, kinda like the Amish except that they use technology and practice birth control. They are the "Yin" to the Amish "Yang." Now there are six Shakers somewhere in Maine and 250,000 Amish! Unlike the replica Amish Village in Pennsylvania, the Hancock Shaker Village used to be a real one. It started in the late 1780s with 100 Believers and by 1830, there were about 300 Believers living in the community. They built communal houses, workshops, and dairy barns. They also cultivated medicinal herbs, vegetables, fruits, and other crops to sustain themselves. The village was called "The City of Peace." Over the years, the community slowly dwindled. The City of Peace, now known as the Hancock Shaker Village, has become a history museum with twenty authentic buildings, a working farm, and a collection of Shaker furniture and artifacts. We were taken on a tour of the buildings by an authentically attired guide. The 1826 Round Stone Barn and the Brick Dwelling are the most prominent ones. A Shaker musical performance in the Brick Dwelling was part of the experience. The Shakers had a very unique way of writing their music scores, resulting in their music having a lilting, soothing quality to it. I promptly fell asleep during the performance and I thank my canine gods that I did not embarrass AC again by snoring in the middle of the show! Maybe you should hear the story of how I embarrassed AC in Stanford a few months before.

I was attending a class in the Law school. In the beginning of the course, the professor announced that dogs are allowed in class. So, I decided to bring Zen along for the next one. Knowing that he can be a pest if he is bored, I took him for a long walk before the class. It was hot and I could see that he was tired. Good, *I thought,* now he will be chill. *I introduced him to the class and he was greeted with a loud, "Hi, Zen."*

He settled down next to me. The class began and in a few minutes, I heard a gentle snore from the side. I looked down and the pup was asleep. Oh God, I hope he doesn't start snoring like he does at home.

My fear came true. The next snore was a few octaves higher than the first one. About three snores into the orchestra, the professor stopped in mid-sentence and said, "Do I hear somebody snoring?" Zen answered that question loudly and topped it off with a satisfied grunt. The class dissolved into laughter peppered with a few "So cute!" comments. Suffice it to say that I never took him to class again.

My gastronomically inclined epicurean humans had another memorable dinner. It was very smelly. The garlic fan in our family, AC again:

On our way back from the Shaker Village to our hotel, I saw a restaurant called The Roasted Garlic. We stopped to take a look at the menu. More than 50% of the items had some form of garlic. I noticed an appetizer called "Whole Roasted Garlic Head." It is a garlic head halved laterally, dipped in olive oil, and baked in an oven. It comes out soft and gooey and flavorful without the bite of a raw garlic. Memories of eating this every day on a cruise a few years earlier had me drooling like Zen. My dad would say that when I am hungry, my eyes are bigger than my stomach. This led me to order two large garlicky appetizers, and as if that was not enough, I added a roasted garlic pizza to the list.

The aftermath of this meal was felt by everyone. Our room smelled of garlic…my hair smelled of garlic…DC smelled of garlic. Only Zen seemed to have been spared. He did keep walking around with his nose in the air, sniffing, attempting to track down the source of this overpowering aroma. The food was delicious and I felt sorry that we couldn't take it in the car next day. We had a long drive to New York.

We hit our first traffic jam on the I-91 about 140 miles from New York. *Welcome back to civilization*, I thought, not very pleasantly. I had fallen in love with the bucolic pace of life for the past week.

For the first time in our journey, our destination was meant to be a mix of work and pleasure. AC had lined up some work meetings and DC and I were supposed to be having some fun on our own. It didn't turn out that way. As we drove toward New York, farmland gave way to suburbia, two-lane highways gave way to four and five-lane expressways. The 55 mph speed limit increased to a 65 mph limit. The laidback atmosphere was giving way to the hustle and bustle of urban living.

The GPS started playing tricks on us as we neared New York.

AC, our navigator, would tell DC, "Keep on this road for the next ten miles. We have to get on the Kennedy Bridge."

The next minute, the GPS lady would say, "Please take the next exit in half a mile."

DC: "So, am I taking the next exit?"

AC: "No. I don't know why this keeps rerouting me. Stay on this road."

GPS lady: "Rerouting you now. Please take the next exit in two miles."

DC (muttering): "*$##** GPS. Let's just ignore it. Look for signs for Kennedy Bridge."

AC: "Okay. Don't get mad. There's the sign for Manhattan."

Once we entered Manhattan, AC knew the lay of the land and we reached our hotel quickly. We were booked in a very fancy dog-friendly hotel called The Pierre. Obviously, I was welcomed in a 5-star way. A lovely white tablecloth and elegant stand with two stainless steel bowls, Fiji bottled water, dog biscuits and all that. Told you my dinners were getting memorable.

The Pierre is on E. 61st Street and 5th Avenue, near the south end of Central Park. As I jumped out of the car, a wave of noise and a cornucopia of smells borne on a warm breeze assailed me. The concrete below my feet was hot; there was an incessant drone of traffic mingling with human voices, interrupted by the wailing siren of an ambulance or the honking of an impatient driver. I could smell horses, the marking signals of other dogs on the walls of the building, smoke, car exhaust, and pizza. Pizza? My head swiveled around to track down this scent. It came from the row of tables set on the sidewalk. I tried to sneak in for a closer look and possibly a bite, but was strongly dissuaded by AC.

My evening walk was in Central Park with hundreds of human legs blocking my vision. Sometimes those legs were accompanied by doggy legs. The park is Doggy Central for the canine citizens of New York. So many dogs to play with. I was beside myself with joy. I scampered and skittered from one bush to the other, getting my leash tangled in tourists' legs. DC positively hated it and for the first time on the trip, I got yelled at. "ZEN! STOP IT." With a quick yank of my leash, I was told to "HEEL." I did that for 30 seconds and took off for another sniff, almost bowling over an old woman.

An aging husky, one of my New Yorker doggy brethren, looked at me aghast. "Another nut from the West Coast!"

"That's it," DC said. "Let's go back to the hotel. This sucks."

So we returned to our palatial room, and after a royal dinner in my gleaming bowls, topped off with a drink of Fiji bottled water, I lay down on my bed in the corner and fell asleep. Sometime later through the fog of sleep, I heard DC saying, "I don't like this place. There is only concrete and Central Park smells like a toilet. There is nothing we can do during the day while you are at work. I can't leave Zen alone in the hotel room and go off to see something. We will go to Andy's place tomorrow and you can join us after your work is done."

And so, the next morning, after an uneventful walk in a less crowded Central Park, DC and I left our 5-star digs and headed off to Andy's home. Despite the luxurious accommodations there, I was only too happy to leave New York. I don't like crowded streets, noisy surroundings, and concrete under my feet. I also dislike doing my jobs on concrete. The wailing sirens kept me up most of the night. It is such a strange disturbing sound. After this experience, I concluded that I am not a big city dog.

PART 4C

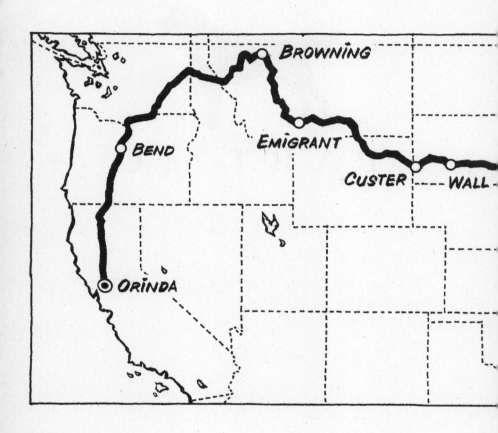

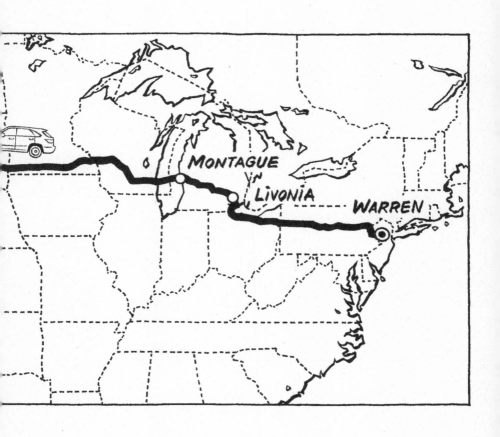

CHAPTER 13

The Horse That Never Was

We commenced our return leg with the longest single-day drive of the trip, a 620-mile, nine-hour, cruise-controlled leap through New Jersey, Pennsylvania, and Ohio that terminated in Livonia, Michigan. The plan was to cross Lake Michigan on a ferry, cut through Wisconsin, skirt the southern edge of Minneapolis on our way to Mount Rushmore, then stop for ten days in Yellowstone National Park and Glacier National Park. The final leg would take us through Idaho and Washington before we swung south through Oregon to get home.

Michigan turned out to be full of pleasant surprises. We visited the University of Michigan at Ann Arbor. In a scene reminiscent of the past, AC was searching for an elusive law school quadrangle and I thought, *Here we go again*. Memories of the "mysterious sculpture in the pond" hunt in Nebraska still haunt me! We did find the quadrangle and it was pretty, or at least it seemed pretty through the scaffolding erected all around it. Looks like the law school was getting a face-lift.

It was a cool, cloudy day and the walk through The Diag was exciting. The Diag is a large open space in the center of the university. Originally known as the Diagonal Green, it derived its name from the walking paths cutting diagonally through it. A big brass "M" is located in the center of the Diag. I happily walked all over it, not knowing the legend: if you step on it as a freshman, you will fail your first exam. Ha! I was a freshman, but school was out.

Lots of squirrels were scurrying around as we walked through the Diag. Unlike the small ones back in Singapore, these were huge; some of them were as big as a cat. They are obviously a central character in university life here. A few years ago, the students formed a Squirrel Club. At some point it was the one of the largest student organizations in the university with over 400 members. After walking on 200-year-old paths, we stepped into the 100-year-old Nickel's Arcade with its eclectic collection of stores and hipster coffee joints. Nestling within the arcade is a quirky cafe called Comet. The coffee at Comet's was decidedly modern, and we sat there drinking in the atmosphere.

A must see in nearby Dearborn is The Henry Ford Museum and Greenfield Village. You would think the Ford Museum would be only about cars, and you would be wrong. It showcases US history around the four *"A*s" in Ford's life: Automobiles (to be expected), Agriculture, Aviation, and Automation. The museum and the Village reflect Ford's education philosophy. He was a firm believer in "learning by doing." The Village was set up as an educational institute where students learned by playing around with everyday objects. In addition, Ford was an avid collector of objects which reflected industrial progress. This collection soon encompassed anything Americana, from artifacts like "Ambler's mowing machine," circa 1836, the oldest surviving American harvester, to a trade sign for G. Smith Boot and Shoe Store, circa 1875. At the ticket booth, AC leaned over and whispered something to the young lady behind the counter. They both looked at DC and me, standing a few feet away. I faintly caught the words, "It's okay as long as he is on the leash." And so, we ambled into the museum—three Californians in the halls of 20th century innovation.

We entered a gigantic hall with large directional signs showing the way to the various collections. I smelled some nice juicy hot dogs and gently pulled DC off to the left. We walked a few feet and I stopped. The hot dog aroma was gone. *Probably a kid with a hot dog in his hand*, I thought. DC was staring at something. I heard the words muttered in an incredulous tone, "Is this really a test tube containing Edison's last breath?

211

That's unbelievable." Who knows whether it really does. Thomas Edison was one of Ford's closest friends. His workshop has been recreated in Greenfield Village, which we would visit later.

We were strolling past a line of shiny cars. Instinctively I thought, *Aha! Maybe I can leave an "I was here" message.* Presciently DC pulled me up short and I behaved. This exhibit was the Presidential Vehicle collection. It has the horse-drawn carriage used by Theodore Roosevelt (1901-1909), the FDR Sunshine Special which is the first car built specifically for presidential use, the open-top limo in which Kennedy was assassinated, and the armored vehicle in which a wounded Ronald Reagan took cover from a madman's bullets.

AC loves guided tours because they are the most efficient way to see the most important exhibits and get a lay of the land. So, we took one. I was the only dog on the tour and the guide, a gentle old man, greeted me with a pat on the head and a "Looks like we have a doggy interested in history" remark.

Our first stop was at a rocking chair that President Lincoln was seated in when he was shot. The guide talked about how the chair was used only for special occasions at the theater and how the large stain is not blood but hair oil. I heard an audible sigh of relief from the group. Moving on from the morbid to a failed promise, we stopped at the aviation section next to a funny-looking plane. Our guide had an interesting story about this contraption. "And here we have the Ford Flivver. How many of you have seen or heard of this plane?" A few hands went up. None of them belonged to my companions!

"Good," he said and continued, "Ford's vision was to make a plane available to every citizen in America. Kinda like the Model T of the air. As you can see, it is very small. It has a little wheel at the back so that the pilot can drive it from home to the nearest makeshift runway. Cool, isn't it?" That got him a few nods and murmurs of appreciation from the group. He continued, "Ford launched it on his birthday in 1926. Any of you kids know Ford's birthday?" he asked. The question did not elicit any response. "It is July 30th." He carried on, "Unfortunately, the project was stopped in 1928. One of the planes crashed in Florida and that was it."

The final stop on the tour was next to a bus. *What's the big deal about a bus?* The guide answered my thought dramatically, declaring, "This is the bus that changed America forever," which drew a lot of oohs and aahs from his captive audience. "This is the bus in which Rosa Parks refused to give her seat to a white man. It's 1955 and segregation is still a practice in Montgomery, Alabama. Parks is arrested and fined ten dollars. In protest, 99% of African Americans in the city boycott the Montgomery Bus service from December 1955. The boycott is successfully led by Martin Luther King. In

November 1956, the Supreme Court declares segregated busing unconstitutional. The rest is history." He paused for dramatic effect.

"With this, we have come to the end of our tour. Thank you for your attention. Feel free to wander about and have a good rest of the day." He ended with a flourish that elicited clapping and thank-yous.

The three of us wandered off to take a look at Ford's other cars. One of them was an electric car that Ford's wife drove. At the beginning of the twentieth century. Bowza! So, me driving around in a Tesla in San Francisco a hundred years later is no big deal!

My nose quivered as I smelled burgers and fries. "Ah. A diner. Let's grab some lunch." The suggestion was not aimed at me, but at AC. DC had seen the source of the appetizing smell: Lamy's Diner. We were in the Driving America section. AC came over and looked at the menu, muttered, "Nothing vegetarian for me here," and walked away. DC and I followed. The three of us sat down on a bench just outside the diner. Well, I was on the floor, they were on the bench. My mind was still screaming "Burgers," but DC was looking around with a contemplative expression. What's going on in that brain? I thought as I fixed my gaze on DC, trying to get in and read the thoughts coursing around inside. Here's what DC was thinking: Hmm, there are signs for Howard Johnson motel, Texaco gasoline pump, and a diner. So, there's food, gas, and a place to stay. We've seen this at every exit on the interstate highways. That makes any road trip much easier.

How did America become a country of drivers?

The inexpensive Ford Model T became wildly popular in the early part of the 20th century. The 1920s saw an exponential growth in automobile ownership and by the end of the decade, 23 million cars were registered. People would drive out to see the countryside, though a trip like that would require extensive planning. There was no place to stay or eat, no mechanics, and the roads were terrible.

In 1919, a young Lt. Colonel by the name Dwight Eisenhower undertook a cross-country trip from DC to San Francisco in a convoy of military vehicles. They made good time till they reached Nebraska. After that, it was an endless series of getting bogged down, breakdowns, ruts, and dirt tracks for roads till they crossed the Sierra Nevadas into California. They reached San Francisco in 62 days. This trip reinforced Eisenhower's belief that an interstate highway system was essential and it had to be managed by the federal government. Thirty-seven years later, when he became President, Eisenhower signed the Highway Act of 1956 and construction began soon thereafter.

As the interstate highways started getting built, more and more Americans started traveling, and the need for gas stations, motels for a quick sleepover, and diners offering the quintessential American food of burgers, fries, and milkshakes became apparent. Small businesses rushed to fulfill this need and over time, travel across America became easy-peasy.

Adjacent to the museum is the outdoor Greenfield Village, an eighty-acre area with seven historic districts that reflect 300 years of American life. One district, called "The Working Farms," shows the agricultural practices of those days, and another one, "Edison at Work," showcases his laboratory and the innovations which led to the development of the light bulb. Then there is "Main Street," which has all the businesses of that period. Some of the restaurants in Main Street serve authentic nineteenth-century food. DC grabbed a frozen custard, definitely not nineteenth century! Vintage Ford Model Ts chug around the village offering rides to visitors. DC, the car buff, wasn't feeling up to it, so we sat on a modern bench on Main Street while AC went for the ride.

Zen wasn't allowed into the Model T, so a hangry (a portmanteau of hungry and angry; irritable due to hunger) DC stayed back with him and I took the tour. I was helped up into the car by the driver, a mustachioed old gentleman,

*wearing what I think is early twentieth century attire: long
coat and a tall hat. The car was noisy and bumpy and open,
but it still was a fun drive. We drove past replicas of historically
significant residences like the first electrified house, the oldest
windmill in the US, and the house where Wright Brothers
grew up. I was sorry when the tour finished. I didn't feel like
meeting a hangry DC. Luckily for me, the frozen custard had
taken the edge off. Hanger had dissolved into a mild acceptance
that the pangs of hunger had to be held off for a few more hours.*

Hanger happens to humans. When I get hungry, I
don't get grumpy. I have two routines that I use on the
humans in my life. One, become a cute pest and bother
both of them individually with intense, penetrating looks
and body rubs and nuzzles that say *"Guys, I am hungry.
Food please,"* till one of them gets the message and feeds
me. If that fails, walk away and lie morosely in a corner
till one of the them notices and realize they haven't fed
me. Unsurprisingly, it is AC who always notices it first,
reinforcing my conviction that we have a special bond.

Montague—the place where DC wanted to live
forever. Our overnight stop was at the Weathervane
Inn in Montague. AC found this inn by sheer luck
(and Expedia, of course). The inn has stunning views
of White Lake. DC was dancing in delight when we
checked into our room on the first floor.

*I woke up with the first light filtering through the crack in
the curtain. Zen stirred as I sat up and quietly padded over to
the balcony door for a quick look. It was 5 AM and AC was fast*

asleep. The sun was peeking out behind our inn. I could see its rays gradually lighting up the marina and the boats like a giant beacon slowly sweeping aside the cloak of darkness. The still waters of the lake became a perfect mirror and I just stood there, entranced, mesmerized by the reflections of the boats, the brilliant white hulls contrasting the deep blue of the water. Magical! Twenty minutes later, I was sitting in the balcony, sipping the first coffee of the day. Zen was sitting at my feet. Ah…this is life, *I thought. I couldn't have asked for a better start to my day. I could stay here forever.*

And…and…I can't wait to tell you this, I met Zuzu on my morning walk. Can you imagine? Another dog whose name begins with Z! I thought I was the only one in the world. She was an eight-year-old dog staying with her humans on the ground floor of the inn. Of course, we had a lot of fun chasing each other and playing bump and run. It was all good till she jumped into the lake for a swim. I almost followed her but was stopped in mid-leap by DC's sharp "STAY." The magic word had its intended effect. I stopped. I would have still followed her again but AC managed to collar me. No fair! (Can you visualize me stomping my paws in protest?) This time I kept my heart locked away.

The Frederik Meijer Gardens and Sculpture Park was an AC must-see site. It has been named after Mr. Meijer, the billionaire founder of the Meijer "hypermarket" chain. He loved sculptures and his wife loved gardens. Combine the billion-dollar net worth with love and you get, arguably, one of the finest sculpture gardens in the world.

The Sculpture Park features almost 300 sculptures spread out across 158 acres. Sculptures and installations by classical artists like Rodin and Degas along with contemporary ones like Henry Moore and Ai Weiwei, the dissident Chinese artist, dot the park. A majority of the works are set outdoors in harmony with the flora. We saw all these works on a tram ride. Dogs are welcome on the tram. My first tram ride. Bowza!

The signature piece is an enormous bronze sculpture, twenty-four feet tall, called "The American Horse." The story behind the sculpture is fascinating. For five hundred years, it was known as "The horse that never was." In 1482, the Duke of Milan commissioned Leonardo Da Vinci to make the world's largest equestrian statue, as a tribute to his father. Da Vinci made a clay model which was destroyed by French soldiers when they invaded Milan in 1499. The work was never completed. Five centuries later, Da Vinci's designs surfaced in a monastery but turned out to be incomplete. Nina Akamu, a famous Japanese animal sculptor, came up with a modified design after carefully researching Da Vinci's sketches. In 1999, she made two full-size casts—one is now at the Hippodrome de San Siro in Milan and the other is here in Michigan. The hoof of that gigantic sculpture was bigger than me.

An installation at the special Ai Weiwei exhibit, called *The Selfie*, is a photo he took on the day he was arrested. Ai Weiwei got into trouble with the Chinese authorities for a piece of art called *Remembering*. He covered the facade of the Hans Der Kunst Museum in Munich with 9,000 backpacks as a memorial to the more than five thousand student deaths in the 2008 Sichuan earthquake. The backpacks, organized by color, shape the letters of one sentence spoken by a victim's mother. According to Weiwei, the deaths were caused by the poor quality of construction and corruption. The Chinese authorities had censored all the news about the deaths, but Weiwei wanted the world to know. Hence his art covering the museum facade. This act led to his arrest in 2009 and the famous photo. AC took a selfie with *The Selfie* and got a big kick out of the idea. Kinda Norman Rockwellish—remember his famous triple self-portrait at the Rockwell museum?

Thanks to AC, I had a memorable visit to a doggy boutique called Decadent Dogs in the small town of Holland. The blackboard said "Bring your humans with you" and I did. The shop had the usual collars, leashes, and clothes for dogs. I find it very weird that dogs wear clothes, especially when they have such beautiful God-given coats and coloring and angel wings! Maybe it is not the dogs. Maybe it is their humans who want to convert them into four-legged humans. Thank God my humans are not like that. The only clothing I have ever worn was the fleece in the snow at Grand Canyon and a raincoat in Palo Alto. The latter because my humans are lazy and don't want to dry me after a walk in the rain.

The "decadent" bit of this store was in the cookie counter. It was well stocked with doggy cookies—Pup Peanut Butter Bars and Corgi Canoli. There was nothing called Lab Snickerdoodle. I would surely have devoured one if it was on the menu. AC bought me a Pup Peanut Butter Bar which I put away in a jiffy.

We crossed Lake Michigan on a comfy Lake Express ferry headed to Milwaukee. Again AC whispered something to the lady at the entry gate and we were allowed to board the ferry first with the kids and physically challenged. We found prime front row seats, with a lot of space in front where I could stretch out and fall asleep without anyone stepping on my tail. My first ferry ride. Bowza! Some of the smells were familiar, like when I was in my crate at the airport or when DC would stop and fill a pungent-smelling liquid into the car. The sound was different, lower in pitch than a plane but higher than Beautè Noire's steady thrum. My ears didn't hurt. This ride was not as scary as my time on airplanes; I could see AC and DC. I relaxed and soon fell asleep. My last awake thought was, *It beats traveling in the cramped confines of the car anytime.*

The Great Lakes can be seen from the moon, and the easiest way to remember their names is HOMES—Huron, Ontario, Michigan, Erie, and Superior. They are also referred to as the inland seas as they have high waves, tides, and beaches, like the sea. Together, they account for 21% of the earth's freshwater supply and 84% of North America's freshwater supply.

CHAPTER 14

The Wild West: Outlaws, Indians, and Bikers

A dream come true—not for me but for DC. Having grown up reading Westerns from bestselling authors like Louis L'Amour and Zane Grey, DC had built this imaginary world of legendary gunfighters, saloons, Injuns (as the writers referred to them in the books), Colt revolvers, and cowboys riding off into the sunset. We were driving through prime Western pulp fiction territory—South Dakota, Wyoming, Montana.

Our next long halt was in Custer, South Dakota, 880 miles away from Milwaukee. We did three overnight halts in this leg of the journey, one in DeForest, one in Mitchell, and the third one in Wall. DC didn't favor overnight halts since that meant consecutive day driving, tiring for all. On this part of the journey, though, we had no choice. We stayed in motels, filled up gas at the station next to the motel, and ate pizza for dinner from the restaurant close by…. Wasn't this the trinity of travel capitalism that made America a country of drivers? As DC said, "Now I know why Americans love to drive."

The summer holidays in my adolescent years were spent reading pulp Westerns. It was my favorite genre by a mile. The vivid scenes of lightning-quick gun draws, the chivalry of the hero cowboys, and the bittersweet feeling of riding off into the sunset without the girl captivated me. The drive along the I-90 adjacent to the sprawling ranches dotted with cattle and even the typeface used on the billboards brought a reality to my imagination. Calamity Jane, Jesse James, Buffalo Bill, are all real! This is the land they rode on and lived in. We stopped in Garretson, a small town with a tourist attraction about Jesse James, the legendary outlaw. As the story goes, James and his gang had unsuccessfully attempted to rob a bank in Northfield, Minnesota. A posse chased him and his gang members to a ravine in Garretson. James jumped his horse across the ravine and escaped from his pursuers. Even for a horse, a twenty-foot jump over a sixty-foot drop is near impossible. In all probability, the good townspeople of Garretson concocted the legend in order to make it a tourist attraction. They named the gorge Devil's Gulch, put a bridge across it, and engraved the story on a plaque near the entrance to the bridge. Road warriors like us visit the site and review it on Expedia, encouraging more visitors.

I accompanied DC across the ravine. Any new place with its new smells and sounds always excites me. There is now a grill walkway on the bridge for the tourists. I could see the sixty-foot drop and it made me very nervous. Taught me not to lead with my nose and to curb my enthusiasm when I smell new places. Stupid dog!

DC had picked the town of Wall as a stop. With a population of 800 and an area of 2.2 square miles, Wall's tourist population vastly outnumbers the locals. Why? It is the gateway to Badlands National Park and the Minuteman Missile Site. More importantly, Wall Drug Store is a destination site. Its handprinted billboards on the I-90 advertising the store catapulted it into an iconic brand. The Wall Drug Store is now a mini shopping mall with restaurants and retail shops staffed by pretty young girls speaking English in strange accents. Apparently, it is a popular summer destination for Eastern European and Russian girls to earn some dollars.

The story behind the road signs that draw two million visitors a year:

In 1936, Wall Drug was your average small-town drugstore. The owners, Dorothy and Ted Hustead, wanted to attract more customers. Dorothy suggested putting up a road sign on Route 16, advertising Wall Drug Store and offering free iced water. The idea was a great success. Ted Hustead then set up similar signs starting twenty miles away, showing the distance to the store. The signs went international when American GIs fighting in WW II

displayed signs in France showing the distance to Wall Drug Store. Ted scored an interview on BBC when he hung a distance sign in the London Underground. The mainstream media got into the act and Wall Drug Store became a tourist destination.
The signs are still hand-painted and free ice water is still available.

Wall is also a stop for all the Harley bikers on their way to the Sturgis Rally. "Bikers welcome" signs were posted in all shops, including cafes. There was an array of bikes parked in the middle of the street. Chrome exhaust pipes flashed in the sunlight. Fuel tanks painted in neon green and garish purple cried "look at me" to the non-biker crowd taking photos with their smartphones. We received strange looks as we squeezed Beautè Noire in an empty slot among the bikes. The tattooed bikers, dressed in traditional leathers emblazoned with the Harley Davidson logo, were wandering about inside the stores. I wondered how the leather-encased bikers handled the summer heat. I was hot in my natural coat. At least I could cool down by sweating through my paws. These guys have thick boots on. You have to be tough to be in the Harley biker club. We did see a smart solution in Garryowen, a few days later. A biker walked into the store dripping water all over the floor. He bought some ice, wrapped it in a soaking wet towel and stuffed it into his helmet. "Keeps me cool," he remarked to the store clerk as he walked out.

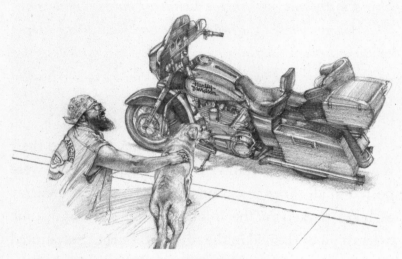

So, what is the Sturgis Rally?

Sturgis, a small town about a hundred miles away from Wall, hosts an annual motorcycle rally which is attended by half a million bikers. They swarm every town within a 200-mile radius. About 80% of the motorcycles are Harley Davidsons. The rest are just…um, bikes. DC remarked that the iconic throbbing beat of a Fat Boy (the bike, not the biker, haha!) gives him goose pimples. It just gives me a headache. The sound is bloody painful to my sensitive ears.

Badlands National Park is 244,000 acres of rugged moonscape beauty carved by millions of years of water and wind erosion. It has one of the richest fossil beds in the world, dating back 23 to 35 million years. Though it is called Badlands, it is inhabited by deer, bison, bighorn sheep, and a variety of mammals. Guess it ain't too bad for them, huh? (You dig the accent?). It was really hot. I jumped out at one place and promptly singed my paws. After that, I stayed back, watching the deer from the cool confines of the car.

The vast emptiness of Wisconsin, Minnesota, and South Dakota is mesmerizing. The I-90 cuts through this green and brown landscape as if a giant hand has drawn a straight black line. I could have kept my hands off the wheel and watched a movie without going off the road. There is a certain awe-inspiring magnificence to the emptiness of this vista, very different from the barrenness of the Salt Flats in Utah. I felt insignificant, but it was liberating. The steady whoosh of the wind rushing past the car and the monotonic hum of tires on the asphalt contrasted with the silence in the car. A cloak of calm control slowly draped me from head to toe. I have never felt anything like it so far. I would never have seen this part of America because it was "fly-over" country. I thanked the gods above for keeping all of us safe and healthy.

Contrary to their name, the Black Hills—the home of Mount Rushmore and Custer State Park—are covered in verdant green trees. "Black Hills" is a translation of the

Lakota word Paha Sapa. Looking through the windscreen of Beautè Noire, they look black and forbidding. Dark clouds shrouded the tops of the hills and rain came pelting down as we neared the foothills. We were driving through a thunderstorm. I wedged myself against the duffel bag. Memories of our near accident were still fresh in my mind. Luckily, there were no exciting incidents and by the time we reached Mount Rushmore, the rain had stopped.

Mount Rushmore is a very impressive monument. Gutzon Borglum, the artist and sculptor, selected George Washington, Thomas Jefferson, Theodore Roosevelt, and Abraham Lincoln to represent the birth, growth, development, and preservation, respectively, of the United States. The carvings were done from 1927 to 1941. The initial plan was to carve statues of the presidents down to their waists, but the project ran out of funds during World War II. Hence only the busts are complete. Incredibly, 90% of the carving was done by dynamiting the rock face.

How did they build Mount Rushmore?

Precisely shaped dynamite charges were inserted into the rock face and detonated till about three to six inches of rock were left for shaping and finishing. Then holes were drilled very close to each other, in a process called honeycombing, so that the small pieces of granite could be removed by hand. Once that was done, hand facers and bumpers were used to smooth the surface to the finish of a sidewalk.

Mount Rushmore has its share of controversy. It is on reservation land managed by the Indians (the original inhabitants of this prairie land and not the South Asian ones). This didn't sit well with the native people and instead of idle protests, Chief Henry Standing Bear commissioned Korczak Ziolkowski, a designer and sculptor who had worked on Mount Rushmore, to assist the local Indian tribes in carving a memorial to their hero, Crazy Horse (more on Crazy Horse will be told when we visit Little Bighorn later). The Crazy Horse Memorial is now the world's largest mountain carving. It is a few miles southwest of Mount Rushmore, on the way to Custer.

Our hotel of choice this time was The Bavarian Inn, a Swiss chalet-style inn with pretty flowers hanging over the entrance and a killer crepe pancake breakfast. That's DC's kind of breakfast. Additionally, DC found a historic coffee shop, the 1881 Bank Coffee House. It is in the building that housed the First National Bank of Dakota Territory, which was established in 1881. Hence the name. The doors and trim are original but the hardwood floor is authentically replicated. Even the ceiling is original tinplate. Coffee is ordered at the teller counter, the baristas make it in the vault, and pick-up is at the withdrawal window. Very cool!

Wildlife Loop Road is a scenic drive in Custer National Park. It is a 18 mile loop where one can expect multiple "wildlife jams." One traffic jam was caused by a herd of bison. They were crossing from one side to the other in a leisurely manner, but stopped on the road for some unknown reason. Traffic came to a halt for over twenty minutes—the only traffic jam that AC and DC actually enjoyed.

I had my fun growling at them. One gargantuan specimen came over to our car for a personal meet and greet and I welcomed him with a fusillade of noise. "Bow Bow.... Boooowoooo BOW Woof BOW!" The bloke didn't blink even though I was at him full on—growls, barks, snarls, the works. AC and DC were frozen in their seats, holding their breath and praying that he wouldn't put dents in the car. He stared inside for a while and then ambled away.

Back at the Bavarian Inn, I made a new puppy friend, Mabel, and we had a wonderful play date. She was really cute and bouncy. We eventually got so tired that we just sat holding hands, or so AC thought, while capturing this "tender moment" for posterity. Dogs don't do "tender moments" and we definitely don't hold hands or paws.... And I kept my heart locked away again. She was too young. Sigh! *Am I ever going to meet another Lynda?* As it turned out, it was not in my fate.

In the middle of the night, I woke up with a feeling that something was crawling around inside my right ear. Scratch! Scratch! Shake! Shake! I shook my head violently, and my ears flapped noisily. Thwack thwack

thwack…. The racket woke up AC. "What's happening, Zen? Why are you scratching your ear?"

Something is in there and I can't get it out. It's very itchy and ticklish. God! Why didn't I get a moveable forefinger to stick inside my ear? Would have been useful right now.

"Hey. Let me see." AC grabbed my head in one hand and upturned my ear with the other. "DC, come here, look at his ear. It is pimply and red."

DC got out of bed and came over to take a look. "Looks like he has an ear infection. Let's clean it and we'll take him to a vet in the morning."

AC got some cotton buds and the ear cleaning solution from my first aid kit (yes, that first aid kit of my own was useful this time). DC grabbed my head and AC squirted the solution into my ear. It felt like someone had jabbed an icicle in there. I wanted to shake it desperately. DC's headlock prevented me from doing so. AC gently cleaned my ear out with the cotton buds. The crawlies inside seemed to quieten down.

Later in the morning, we drove to Southern Hills Animal Clinic, a few miles east of Custer on Route 16A. There, a friendly vet diagnosed it as a yeast infection. Yuck! What was yeast doing in my ear? The vet said that I could have picked it up anywhere in the last few days and it is a typical malady in traveling dogs. The other thing she said was to watch out for an upset stomach, another common affliction with road-tripping pooches. She dispensed an antibiotic with instructions to drop it in both my ears twice a day. We were on our way after a couple of hours.

"The only good Indian is a dead Indian." – General Philip Sheridan in 1869 during the Indian Wars.

Indigenous peoples were already present for millennia before the first European colonizers set foot on the North American continent. Estimates suggest that the native population was between seven to ten million before the arrival of Columbus. They were grouped into approximately six hundred tribes, the large ones being the Cherokee, Iroquois, Apache, Comanche, and Pequot. Some tribes were primarily agriculturists, like the Cherokee, while the Apache were nomadic hunter-gatherers. A clash of civilizations was inevitable between the Christian Anglo-Saxon colonizers and the Native Americans. Large-scale armed conflict, popularly referred to as the "Indian Wars," took place between the Indians and the colonizers pre-Independence, and between the US Government and the Indians post-Independence. The wars ended in the late nineteenth century with the massacre of 300 Sioux at Wounded Knee Creek in 1890. In 500 years, the native population had declined to 238,000.

Andrew Jackson was a firm believer in "Indian removal." In his annual address to Congress in 1833, Jackson denounced Indians, stating, "They have neither the intelligence, the industry, the moral habits, nor the desire of improvement which are essential to any favorable change in their condition. Established in the midst of another and a superior race...they must necessarily yield to the force of circumstances and ere long disappear." As an Army general, he had led campaigns in Georgia, Alabama, and Florida to transfer Indian landholdings to white settlers. When he became president, he continued this removal even more actively. In 1830, he signed the "Indian Removal Act." This gave the federal government authority to remove all the Indians east of the Mississippi to a new packet of land in what is now Oklahoma. In the decade of the 1830s, approximately 100,000 Cherokee were forced to relocate to the West. More than 15,000 died in what is tragically but eloquently referred to as the "Trail of Tears."

Another tragedy was to play out forty-five years later at the Battle of the Little Bighorn in Montana. This battle was the most consequential one in the Great Sioux War (1876-1877). The war, sparked by the discovery of gold in the Black Hills, was marked by a series of battles in Montana, Wyoming, Nebraska, and South Dakota between the Sioux and the US Army. The US Army blatantly ignored a treaty established earlier and invaded the Black Hills, a sacred area for the Lakota

Sioux, to allow white prospectors and settlers access to the gold. This upset the Sioux and they took up arms. In the spring of 1876, two respected Sioux chiefs, Sitting Bull and Crazy Horse, assembled tens of thousands of warriors on the banks of the Little Bighorn River. The stage was set for an epic clash. The battle took place on June 22, 1876. The US Army, led by General Custer, suffered its worst defeat of the Indian Wars. An Indian force numbering about 3,000 annihilated Custer's 7th Cavalry. Custer and 215 of his men died on that fateful afternoon.

Three days after the Battle of Little Bighorn, there were reports that one of Custer's staghounds, Tuck, was found sitting next to his body. She had been blinded in the left eye by a bullet but otherwise seemed uninjured.

This could have been her story of the battle:

My head hurts but I cannot leave my master, my beloved master. I know he is gone.

I was his favorite. In a letter to his wife, he wrote, "Did I tell you of Tuck catching a full-grown antelope-buck, and pulling him down after a run of over a mile, in which she left the other dogs far behind? She comes to me every evening when I am sitting in my large camp chair . . . First she lays her head on my knee, as if to ask if I am too much engaged to notice her. A pat of encouragement and forefeet are thrown lightly across my lap; a few moments of this posture and she lifts her hind feet from the ground, and great overgrown dog

*that she is, quietly and gently disposes of herself on my lap . . .
She makes up with no other person."*

He was a Civil War hero, one of the youngest generals in
the Union Army, earning him the nickname "Boy General." An
imposing six feet tall, with a brash, almost fatalistic attitude,
he was reputed to be a brilliant cavalry tactician, always at
the head of his troops. After the Civil War ended, General
Pershing deputed him to lead the Seventh Cavalry in the
Indian Campaign in the Great Plains. He loved dogs and
always had more than a few with him on his campaigns. We
would hunt antelope, buffalo, rabbit, and other wild animals
on the plains of Dakota.

Comanche, his favorite horse, and I were his protector
animal spirits as he charged at the enemy. Alas, we both failed
to protect him three days ago.

We had left Fort Lincoln in pursuit of a band of Lakota,
Dakota, and Cheyenne Indians. The dry summer heat of
Dakota Territory made the going slow and laborious. A few
days later, we arrived in Little Bighorn Valley. Our scouts
had determined that the Indians were camped along the Little
Bighorn River and did not know we were approaching. The
terrain—low hills, valleys, and the tall summer grass—
favored the attackers. My master planned a three-pronged
attack, two groups attacking from the southeast while he
would attack with the third column from the northwest.

As he moved along a low ridge running parallel to the
encampment, he realized that it was much larger than what the
scouts had told him. There were at least 6,000 Indians, men,

*women, and children, camped along the river. They saw our
column approaching and the warriors attacked us immediately.
Fully aware that he was outnumbered and outgunned, my
master ordered a retreat up a small hill that will go down in
history as Last Stand Hill. He hoped the upslope defensive
position would help him hold off the Indians till reinforcements
arrived. He was so wrong. He couldn't see the Indians because
they were attacking on foot, crawling out of sight in the tall
grass, popping up yelling ferociously, firing bullets and arrows,
swinging tomahawks. I could smell them and hear them. It
was vicious close quarter combat, where I was one of the few
well equipped for it—big teeth, sharp reflexes honed from years
of hunting, and eighty pounds of muscle. The soldiers were
carrying single shot rifles and no swords, putting them at a
material disadvantage to the Indians with their repeater rifles
and tomahawks. I charged at an Indian warrior, snarling with
bared teeth. I could taste his blood as my teeth sank into his neck
and tore his throat apart. He went down without a sound. I
turned, ducked a swinging tomahawk, and buried my teeth
into another torso, ripping out a bloody chunk of flesh. There
was so much noise around me, men screaming in pain, my
master shouting orders, guns firing and smoke everywhere. I
never left his side. Anyone that came within range of my jaws
was brought down. Suddenly, I felt a sharp pain in my head
as something hit my left eye and I went down with a loud
yelp. I could taste blood. It was streaming out from my eye and
I couldn't see anymore. I turned my head and saw my master*

get hit in the head and fall. Comanche was already down and I didn't know if he was still alive.

After a while, the screaming and the noise subsided and a hush settled over the hill. The smell of death hung in the air. Two hundred and ten soldiers met their end with my master. I found him lying on his side, blood flowing from his head and staining his uniform, his eyes staring into nothingness—those same eyes that would look down on me fondly as I nuzzled him. He died a hero fighting alongside the men he led. I lay down next to him, ignoring my own pain, and that's how they found us three days later. I had failed to protect him.

Here is a happier story from DC about our time in Montana:

One of the more enduring memories from all the Western fiction I read was of the guns that the characters used in the story. Colt, Winchester, Springfield were familiar names to me. I got an opportunity to be up close and personal with a Springfield at the Custer Battlefield Museum in Garryowen, Montana. The town with a population of two has been named after the Irish song that Custer adopted for the Seventh Cavalry's marching tune. It has a gas station, a convenience store, and the museum. Chris Kortlander, the owner of Garryowen and the museum, is an avid historian. He bought this parcel of land in 1993 after his house in Malibu burned down in a fire and set up the museum with his own funds. It is built on Chief Sitting Bull's campsite and it is adjacent to one of the few US monuments outside Arlington National Cemetery that is dedicated to an unknown soldier. In 1926, Sitting Bull's nephew and General Godfrey, who was a lieutenant at the Battle, buried a real hatchet to signify lasting peace and to honor the dead on both sides. Now I understand the etymology of "bury the hatchet." Historically hatchets were buried by chiefs of Indian tribes to signal peace and an end to the conflict.

The museum has some very unique pieces from that era, including Chief Sitting Bull's battle headdress; a collection of letters written by Custer to his wife, Libbie; and an original 1857 Springfield carbine used by a Crow scout at the battle. Chris kindly allowed me to hold the weapon. I was over the moon. AC captured the image for posterity. In it, you can see me grinning like a fool.

People like Chris epitomize the passion and commitment of Americans to preserve the history and legacy of America so that it can be passed on to the next generation and the next.

CHAPTER 15

Hiss, Pop, Crackle: Sounds of Yellowstone

O ur first contact with Yellowstone was magical. It had just stopped raining around us and the sky was overcast in patches. On the horizon, we saw a fiery spire, a giant yellow, orange, and red ribbon of flame shooting into the clouds. A patch of rain in the distance had caught the setting sun at the right angle and set off this awesome display. Yellowstone couldn't have welcomed us in any better way.

Yellowstone is the world's first national park and it is humongous, more than 3,000 square miles across three states with 500 active geysers and three to four million visitors annually. It is a geothermal hotspot that quakes and trembles over 3,000 times year. Despite that, flora and fauna flourish in this ecosystem. In nature's ultimate paradox, plants and animals coexist in complete harmony with life-threatening geysers and gases. The park's terrain was formed when three volcanoes blew up about two million years ago and formed three giant calderas. The largest is 45 by 30 miles. Yellowstone has a hotspot at a very shallow depth, which acts like a giant blowtorch causing the bubbling of mud, eruption of geysers, and all the other dramatic stuff associated with geothermal activity. Old Faithful is one such geyser, which erupts on cue every ninety minutes or so. And here I thought only dogs were faithful.

We stayed in a spacious cabin at Camel Discovery Ranch, in the middle of nowhere—which kinda describes life in Montana. The nearest neighbor was half a mile away. The cabin was large, new, and very comfortable. It was about a mile from the highway, halfway up a hill, accessible only by a dirt road. There was a barn and a large fenced-off area to one side.

Jason greeted us on our arrival. He had long hair and a wild beard. He was also wearing a beanie in the middle of summer. Despite his odd appearance, he loved dogs and we bonded instantly. I was soon lying on my back with a goofy grin, paws waving ecstatically, getting a stomach rub. Heavenly!

Jason turned out to be quite an interesting person. He was an animal trainer. I could make that out by the way Zen greeted him. He was also a cinematographer for National Geographic. He had set up a camel ranch near Austin,

Texas, to protect the gene pool of the Asiatic Bactrian camel, a double-humped camel from Central Asia that was facing the threat of extinction. It can survive in extreme heat or cold and dry conditions. Despite its hardiness, the Bactrian camel population is declining, even in the wild. The barn next to our cabin housed eight camels. Two of them were double humped. Zen was looking at them, puzzled, sniffing the air repeatedly with furrowed brows like he usually does when he can't figure out something.

I thought camels originated in the Middle East and India. I also associated them with being inhabitants of the desert. What were they doing in Montana? According to Jason, camels lived in North America forty to fifty million years ago. They were much smaller than their present-day descendants. Fossils can still be found in the valleys near Yellowstone. He had seen a few. I was very surprised.

I was reunited with AC's nephew, Rocky, and his family. They joined us in Yellowstone and would continue traveling with us to Glacier National Park. Rocky's dad, Kris, was an easygoing person who loved dogs. Rocky's mom, Rita, tolerated dogs. I always had short conversations with Kris. He would walk up to me and say, "Zen buddy, what's up?" My response to him usually involved a big tail wag and a full body rub against his leg while he laughingly pummeled me. Rita, on the other hand, was not the chatty type and she chose to ignore me most of the time.

The family was vegetarian and that meant fewer options for food in a restaurant, in this land of red meat. Dinner was cooked in the cabin together in a communal fashion. We had to raid the nearest supermarket, fifteen miles away in Livingston, to stock up on groceries and junk food. This, of course, was only for the humans. My food truck, Beautè Noire, was parked outside.

The cabin had a great outdoors with deer and hare to chase and rattlesnakes to avoid. Jason had warned DC to keep me away from the edge of the trail in late afternoons and early evenings to avoid getting bitten. Well, the city slicker that I am, I almost stepped on one.

DC wasn't paying attention and I was sniffing around behind a small bush. I heard a panicked shout— "ZEN!"—and felt a hand on my collar yanking me away. *Whoa! What happened here?*

I heard DC breath a huge sigh of relief and the word, "Rattlesnake." Lucky for me, the snake was comatose from too much sun and didn't strike.

By the way, did you know there is a rattlesnake vaccine for dogs? Given that three hundred thousand dogs and cats get bitten by snakes every year, getting vaccinated against snake bite makes sense. However, the jury is out on the efficacy of the vaccine.

The next morning, Zen and I met an elderly gentleman strolling along with a massive Lab. That dog was at least one foot taller than Zen. They must make 'em huge in Montana, *I thought. He was our nearest neighbor and he also was from Texas. That's two people I had met so far and they both were from Texas. What is with Texans and Montana? He told me that this was his summer home. They spent March to September in the cool climes of Montana when it was a hundred degrees in Texas.*

We got chatting about bears and snakes and hiking in Yellowstone. He had a "rule of three" bit of advice which I found very surprising. He said that you should always hike in Yellowstone as a threesome.

"Why?" I asked.

"Well, grizzlies never attack threesomes!" he said.

I gave him an incredulous look, thinking, Yeah, right. Like bears can count! *Imagine a bear playing eeny-meeny-miny-mo in his head:* Oh...which one should I attack tonight? But there's three targets here. This one, that one or the one cowering behind...this one.... No...that one.... Ah!... I am confused...I'll just amble away!

He saw my look and said, "Got ya, just kidding."

Yellowstone National Park has 466 miles of scenic routes. Most of them are small mountain roads, curvy, bumpy, sometimes with sharp hairpin bends, all contributing to a very uncomfortable ride at the back. It took a lot of fortitude to keep my lunch in! Lunch was usually a hurried affair in the back of the car. Dinner was a different matter. I had many scenic dinners in Yellowstone, courtesy of AC. One was on the lawns near the visitor center, with Mammoth Hot Springs in the background. The wind was blowing hard enough to make my ears flap around, making it a scenic but uncomfortable meal. Another one was on the shores of Lake Yellowstone at a height of 7,000 feet above sea level. This dinner venue was probably the highest of my life so far. The lake was freezing, as I discovered when I went toe-dipping in the waters after my meal. Dipping toes in Gardiner River, though, was more pleasant! While AC toe-dipped at a point upstream, where cold water from the Gardiner River meets the Boiling River hot springs, one of the few legal soaking areas in Yellowstone, I dipped mine just a few hundred meters downstream in cold but not freezing water.

Watching the sunset in the lush Hayden Valley was also captivating. So many beautiful sights, so little time. Yellowstone was a smorgasbord of sights, smells, and sounds, the familiar and the unfamiliar: sulfurous geysers, camels, elks, and my old friend, the bison. We stopped next to one. This time, I was smarter and just gave it a withering stare. No point wasting my breath on this guy.

We almost hit an elk one evening on a curving mountain road. The sudden stop threw me into the back of the seat among flying Pringle boxes. Unlike their deer cousins, elk don't freeze in the headlights of a car. This one decided to stop and stare down DC.

We had been in Yellowstone for four days and hadn't seen a grizzly. Jason told us to drive to a B Bar Ranch in the mountains. "It's a place only locals know," he whispered conspiratorially to DC. "They come there to feast on huckleberries." He drew a map on the back of a napkin and said, "You can't miss it. There is a big sign that says B Bar Ranch. Be there around 7 PM. That's when they come out to eat."

Off we went, following his map. A single-lane potholed road took us up into the hills. The GPS lady abandoned us just when we needed her, in the middle of nowhere. We pulled over and parked near a horse ranch which looked like bear country. There was no B Bar Ranch sign and nobody else was parked, so we figured we were in the wrong place. After waiting a few minutes and seeing only horses and cows, AC was ready to ask for directions the old-fashioned way. A couple of ranch hands on an ATV were waved over and asked:

"Hey there, where is B Bar Ranch?"

"Drive up this track for a couple of miles and you will see the sign and the parked cars."

We found the ranch and the parked cars. *So much for Jason's "Only the locals know,"* I thought. The grizzles frequented a meadow a mile away and all of us were watching for any sign of movement. I couldn't see them, hear them, or smell them. We waited there for an hour, but no grizzlies. There was a herd of deer and some cattle wandering about and we saw a lone fox crossing the meadow. The bears were taking a break. Maybe they had gorged on too many berries the previous day. All we got for our effort were some deer mooning me! The gall of it.

A few days later, AC had an exciting encounter with a grizzly mom and her cub, in Glacier National Park.

CHAPTER 16

Glaciers and Grizzlies

The clan left the well-appointed cabin in rural Montana and drove to another, differently appointed "cabin" in even more rural northern Montana. Teri, the owner of the cabin, had to be convinced that we, including me, were not going to trash her house. It was listed on Home Away as a pet-friendly location, but Teri was wary of giving it to guests with pets who would, as she said, "treat the cabin as a kennel and a pet toilet." We sent her my best-looking photo and a link to the blog that AC and DC were publishing on our trip so far. She was sold.

When we reached her cabin, she came to meet this "blogger Zen dog." The cabin was more like a ranch house. It was a few miles from the entrance to Glacier National Park. The brick and red-painted wooden structure had a well-kept lawn and a pretty flower bed in the front. Its earlier incarnation was as a rural B&B or hotel or something. It had the full works—an industrial kitchen with a drawer full of professional chef knives, pots and pans to feed fifty people, a dining room for the same number of people, and a small reception area with comfortable sofas in the middle. Old-fashioned book cabinets lined the walls. A glass door opened onto the deck at the back. The bedrooms were tiny; one on the ground floor had a small double bed and a very tiny bathroom. The second one was just above the reception area and the kitchen. It could sleep four and had a slightly larger bathroom. The cabin seemed to be hand-built; large gaps could be seen in all the inner doors and the walls seemed to be off-center. The backyard bordered an RV campground park, beyond which was Teri's small ranch. She and her husband lived on the banks of a little river with their three dogs and twenty dairy cows. How do I know? I met all of them on my morning walk. We also met other neighbors on our evening walk.

Zen and I decided to walk to the RV camp in the evening. The campgrounds were occupied by a motley mix of large and small RVs. And there were there some interesting characters there.

A large towable RV with sides extended to add more bedroom space was parked in a lot. A canopy hung over one side, under which a bearded man was lounging shirtless in his camp chair with a beer in his hand. We walked up to meet him or rather, Zen trotted over to meet him.

"Hi there, buddy! Who are you?" the man said, looking at Zen, who had beaten me to the intro.

"Hi. This is Zen and I'm DC."

"Hi. I'm Roy," he said while heaving himself out of the chair to shake hands. The handshake was firm and friendly.

"Hey, you are a good boy," he said to Zen, who was gamboling around him. "Are you parked in here?" he asked me.

"No. We are in the cabin over there. Just drove in from Yellowstone."

"Ah. Long drive!"

"Yeah, but comfortable. Took a lunch stop in Helena. Quite nice," I said.

All this while, loud barks were coming from inside the RV. "Those are my Labs. Have three of them in there. Is it okay if I let them out to play with Zen?"

"Sure. He loves to play."

Roy sauntered over to the RV door. After opening it carefully, he let himself in and closed it behind him. The barking subsided. In a couple of minutes, he opened the door and came out with three Labs straining at their leashes. One quick word, "Sit," and they all sat. He let them off one by one and they each charged toward Zen, who promptly joined the milling mass of noses and tails. After the introductory sniffing and smelling, they took off in their usual game of chase and catch, hurtling around the campgrounds.

In the course of the conversation, Roy mentioned that he and his girlfriend Gloria occupied two RVs with their five dogs. Yes, five dogs. Roy had three Labradors, the oldest being thirteen and the youngest one two years old, and Gloria had two little ones, both mixed heritage. Roy was an advertising executive in his mid-fifties who had grown tired of the endless client and creative briefings and deadlines. His solution was to sell his apartment in New York, buy an RV, and take off to see America. He had been on the road for seven years and loved it. His plan was to spend the summer near Glacier National Park and move south at the beginning of winter. He had added the dogs in the course of his travels.

One of the Labs ran off toward another RV parked in the adjacent slot. "He's gone to look for Pickles," said Roy. "He is Gloria's dog." Just as he finished the sentence, the RV door opened and a blonde stepped out with a little dog in her arms. "That's Gloria. Hey Glo, come on over and say hi to DC."

"Hi there, I am Gloria. Hi, DC. Meet Pickles," she said, pointing to the little dog.

Gloria would have been attractive in her younger days. The years had not been kind to her. I thought she was in her sixties, but her face was wrinkled beyond her years, though her lips still had the youthful pout. She was as tall as Roy but much bigger everywhere else. The wavy blond hair was swirling around in an unkempt fashion. She let Pickles down and the little guy promptly charged off to join the herd of Labs cavorting around.

"Are you parked here?" she asked me.

"They are in the cabin," said Roy. "Drove over from Yellowstone earlier."

"Yellowstone is pretty, isn't it?" said Gloria. "I was there last year and we loved the sunsets. Such glorious ones. Breathtaking." After a moment of quiet reflection, as if she was reliving the sunsets, she continued, "I have been on the road for the last ten years. I've been all over the US and have seen some beautiful sunsets, but none of them beat the ones in Yellowstone. I think I am done now."

"Why's that?" I asked.

"I'm getting old and think I need a more solid, larger house. Something that doesn't move every time I sneeze."

Roy let out a howl of laughter when he heard that. "You are so funny, Glo. It moves when you dance as well. Haha."

"Where will you settle?" I asked.

"Palm Springs, I think. That's near LA. I like the dry air and I can afford to buy a small house there. With a small garden. Roy can live with me if he wants…or not." The last words came out slowly, accompanied by a sideways glance at Roy. They definitely have had some heated discussions on this topic, I thought.

As we were chatting, a tall figure strode over with a pup on a leash. Her name was Gigi—the pup, that is. She was an Anatolian shepherd mix and at three months old weighed twenty pounds or so. Ivan, the tall guy, was working as part of a road repair crew. Apparently, he had been there for the last nine months while they were working on the road and he and Gigi shared a small RV parked a few slots away. Out of curiosity, I asked him what the crew did in the winter months. Montana winters are extreme and working in a freezing blizzard is definitely not fun. Ivan said that all he did was walk out in the morning to check that the "Road work" sign was not snowed under or blown away by the *wind. And he did that all winter, from late November to early March. He adopted Gigi to keep him company. During the summer months, he would tie her up outside the RV and the other campers would look after her. RV community at its best. I found the whole concept fascinating.*

In the meantime, little Gigi was mixing it up with the Labs and Pickles, and she was holding her own.

I let Gigi bully me. I play very gently with all little ones, carefully, so that my eighty-pound bulk doesn't flatten them at any time. Gigi, though, was a different kettle of fish. She wasn't that big, except in her head. She took a fancy to my ears and would launch herself like a missile at my head and grab one. Owzaa! Those needle-like puppy teeth hurt! Just as I managed to shake her off and trot away, incoming…and bang!…there she was again, hanging from an ear. She was a bundle of energy and could have gone on forever. After about an hour of romping around, I was ready to retire for the night.

Post breakfast next morning, we all piled into one car and headed off to Glacier National Park. This park is a contrast to Yellowstone. It is smaller, about half the size. It has 25 glaciers now. In 1850, it had about 150 of them, but time and global warming had taken their toll. Yellowstone moves and shakes and hisses and moans; Glacier has been rock steady for thousands of years with nary a sound other than the oohs and aahs of visitors admiring the landscape. Yellowstone is spread across three states. Glacier sprawls into Canada. The Canadian border is so close that Alberta Tourism has an office in West Glacier town. Even the air is different—no smell of sulfur, just 100% pure alpine air. SNIFFFFF.... AAAH! Nice! My nose was in the air a lot of the time. Rocky called me a snooty dog. "Zen, you have an attitude," he would say.

During the Ice Age, only the peaks of the mountains were visible above the glaciers. That meant the ice was 5,000 feet deep. Bowza!

Glaciers carve U-shaped valleys or gorges, unlike rivers, which carve more sharp gorges like the Grand Canyon.

The must-do drive in Glacier National Park is called "Going-to-the-Sun." It is a scenic 50-mile road that hugs the mountains on one side with fearsome drops on the other. It winds and meanders through some of the most eye-popping, heart-skipping scenery.

There is an interesting story about this road. It opened in July 1933 after thirty years of construction. The road was designed by a Swiss engineer and the killer app feature, as we say in California, is that it merges so well with the mountainside that it is barely visible. It uses straight stretches of road and fewer switchbacks, which means that it can be open for more months and more people can enjoy driving on it. My humans enjoyed the drive so much that they drove up and down this road, not once, not twice, but thrice. I was not a happy puppy! Only expressways make me happy. Smooth and straight so that I can snooze peacefully. All the starts and stops don't work for me, especially since I was not allowed to disembark at most of them. Hmmph!

We did all our driving in Glacier and Yellowstone, with the clan in what I had designated as the "house car." Kris had rented a giant car, similar to the one DC had on our Yosemite trip. I was sharing my bedroom in the back with a well-stocked human food pantry. Boy, can they eat!!! Since the whole clan except DC were vegetarian, we had to carry a lot of junk food, like Pringles and other assorted unhealthy fried stuff. Rita had packed a few cheese sandwiches as well. Rocky would sneak me bits of those when nobody else was looking.

I went on my first-ever sunset cruise on Saint Mary Lake, one of the many glacial lakes in the park and the site of another one of my scenic dinners. Our guide-cum-boat-captain was a cute young lady from Ohio. I, of course, garnered all her affection. She talked about the forest fires and how they were nature's way of renewing the forest, the geology of the park, and other mundane stuff till we saw a bear walking along the lakeshore. All the humans craned their necks to look at my cousin species ambling along until he or she disappeared into the trees. Young Captain Lady also told us that the grizzly bears here were smaller than their Alaskan cousins because they prefer the succulent and seasonal huckleberries to the fish in the lake. One of nature's mysteries. I would eat the fat lake trout any day.

We had our fair share of excitement on this trip. Rocky and Kris went off trekking, looking for a "Hidden Lake." Unlike all the other mysterious sites on our trip, this one was well marked, just a few miles and a couple of thousand feet lower down the mountain. They did not return for a good four and a half hours. Well...they were supposed to be back in three. Their delayed return caused Rita all sorts of stress. I could sense her discomfort from the back. The tension was oozing out of every pore in her body and hung like a dark cloud over her. I wanted to help her but she wasn't very dog friendly yet, so I kept away. Kris got an earful when they returned. Her mood improved listening to Rocky chattering away about the grizzlies, mountain goats, and bison they had spotted on the trek.

AC had also gone off on another trail and came back breathless and agitated.

It was around two in the afternoon; the sun was shining and it was a beautiful day. Kris and Rocky had gone off earlier. We were sitting in the car and I was getting bored. I decided to go for a walk all by myself on Hidden Lake Trail. It sounded mysterious and fun. I enjoy walking alone, then I don't have to deal with DC the whiner (who hates walking). Zen is a great walking companion but he wasn't allowed on any trails.

The trailhead is just behind the Logan Pass Visitor Center and the round trip is about six miles. I had no intention of going all the way to the lake. The map indicated a midpoint from where I could see the lake and take a few photos. As I started walking, I noticed a sign: "WARNING. Grizzlies are dangerous. Carry bear spray when on the trail." I got a bit worried as I wasn't carrying any bear spray, but there were lots of people and kids walking along, so I felt relieved. Safety in numbers, *I thought.*

I reached the lake viewing point, took a few photos, and briefly contemplated whether I should start walking back. It had been a very pretty walk so far, so I decided to go a bit further. I started strolling downhill admiring the scenery around me. There was a meadow on the right. A couple of hikers were walking about fifty feet ahead of me. They were taking photos when they suddenly stopped and froze, looking at something directly ahead. I stopped and looked around.

Bear! A grizzly and her cub were standing in the middle of the trail and looking at us. The two hikers promptly started to take a "wefie" with the bears in the background. Stupid millennials. So typical, *I thought. Not to be outdone, I quickly took a few photos, not "wefies," and started walking back.*

Meanwhile, the bear and her cub had begun ambling along the trail toward us. Stealing a quick glance behind, I speed-walked up the hill. The hikers trotted past me. "I suggest you run," *I heard one say.*

I am not wearing running shoes, *was the utterly random thought that crossed my mind. I turned and looked back to see if I was going to become bear food. No bear. The trail was empty.* Where did they go? *My breathing was ragged and my heart was pounding from fear and the exertion of speed-walking uphill.*

After a couple of minutes, my breathing slowed and my heart stopped trying to escape from my body. I continued walking, keeping a sharp lookout for the mom and her cub. The trail curved around a bend. And there she was again! She had cut through the meadow on her way up the hill. I could see the cub a few feet behind her. She couldn't have been more than twenty feet away. I froze. She looked at me and sniffed the air. Should I turn and run? Should I shout for help? When will DC come looking for me?

Mama Bear took one last look at me and ambled away. Whew! That was close, *I thought. I waited a few minutes and took off.*

A few minutes later, I crossed two armed forest rangers heading toward where the bear was spotted. They told me to keep going FAST.

Later, when I recounted this story to DC, instead of sympathy at my near-death experience, all I got was a smart aleck comment: "Lucky for you the grizzlies here are vegetarian."

Since we were on a "first" everything—first bear sighting and chase, first campsite buddies, and first lake cruise—my human clan felt compelled to do their first trail ride on horses. Everyone had a different reason to be on a horse: Rita because she had never been on one, Kris because Rita needed moral support, Rocky because he just loves it, and AC having read about all the handsome cowboys in Montana (in the Mills & Boon teenage romance novels). DC and I watched them go from the carpark. As I heard on their return, the ride was boring. Rita's horse refused to obey her. Their butts were sore, and to top it all, the guide was a cowgirl! AC was very disappointed.

Another first was my "birthday" celebration, August 15th. I got a "likka" of rainbow birthday cake ice cream. I was now two years old. Born in Australia, celebrated my first birthday in Singapore, and the second one in America. Where will I be for my third birthday?

CHAPTER 17

Lost in the Haze

We parted ways with Rocky and his family on a Sunday morning with a future promise of more holidays together. The parting was more emotional for my humans. Over the last few days, the two families had developed a deeper relationship. My bedroom went off in the other car, so I was now back to my little space in the back of Beautè Noire. Two more stops, one in Washington and the other one in Portland, and we would be home. After two months on the road and many memorable experiences, a house with a giant backyard and a friendly doggy neighbor awaited my imminent arrival. I was looking forward to sleeping in my Zen Cocoon, going for walks on familiar trails, meeting my cuz and my buddies. Home had a special place in my heart. We bid a fond farewell to Gigi and Gloria and

Roy and cut through the park, savoring its beauty one last time.

Once we were past Glacier National Park, the towering massifs gave way to greener rolling hills. Driving on Montana Highway 35, I saw many signs advertising Flathead cherries. What's a flathead cherry? I wondered aloud. I got no response. AC was fast asleep. Orchards lined the slopes and we discovered what "Flathead cherry" meant. It was not a cherry with a flat top, but cherries from the Lake Flathead region. We also found the elusive huckleberry. In Glacier National Park, the shops were selling huckleberry ice cream, huckleberry jam, and huckleberry beer. The fruit was nowhere to be seen in the stores. Only the bears were supposedly eating the real berries. I was convinced that they were a myth, till we rolled past a town called Big Fork. Now that was Huckleberry Central. The road was lined with little stalls and shops selling huckleberries. They were not a myth. I snared a small basket for a princely sum of $20. That was more expensive than the figs at my farmers market in Palo Alto. A huckleberry is smaller than a blueberry and quite similar in taste. After hunting high and low for them through Montana and paying an exorbitant sum, we spotted them growing wild outside our hotel in Spokane.

The hot afternoon wore off into a warm evening in the mountains of Idaho. The I-90 weaved its way through the spectacular mountain ranges of the Coeur d'Alene National Forest. At the southwestern edge of the forest lies Lake Couer d'Alene. The waters were shimmering in the sunset. Deep, fiery orange rays of a setting sun bounced off the aquamarine water, creating an ethereal vista. We took a detour on a scenic byway to watch a memorable sunset.

The next day was Eclipse Monday in Spokane, and thanks to DC's planning skills we had missed the totality band by a couple of hundred miles! Anyway, we trotted off to Riverfront Falls in downtown Spokane to watch the partial eclipse. DC thought the sky would darken and the birds and animals would fall silent. None of that happened. The sky darkened like at twilight and it got a bit cold...that's all. The birds were merrily chittering away and I heard dogs barking. The animals in Spokane had missed the memo on total silence.

In the US, there are three towns with identical names to cities in India:

1. *Madras , Oregon*
2. *Salem—in 26 states.*
3. *Calcutta, Ohio*

On our way to Bend, we passed through a town called Madras. They have a Madras here, I thought. This was the erstwhile name for Chennai in India. I was surprised that Oregon has another town called Salem, which is also a city in India. This was like the towns in New England. The origin of the names there is clear. In Oregon, it is still a mystery.

The horizon changed as we entered Oregon. We were greeted by a haze that blotted out the scenery. It was familiar to me. The haze had disrupted life in Singapore in 2015. There it was caused by palm plantation fires. AC and I didn't know the cause for this one. We discovered later that it was the smoke from hundreds of forest fires caused by lightning storms a few days prior to our arrival. Apparently this phenomena has been occurring for the past few years. I was very disappointed as I knew it meant that we may have to shorten the rest of the trip. AC doesn't do well in hazy conditions, breathing problems and all that. The sun could be seen as a blurry red ball though all that smoke. It was having a rough few months. First, the moon blocked out its rays for a while; now the smoke was blocking it out as well. It looked very picturesque, though.

Sunriver Resort in Bend was the only bright spot in an otherwise gloomy evening. It's like a small city, with lots of retail and dining, multiple golf courses, and many rooms. We were given a ground floor room with a patio. The room was very comfortable and the patio super comfortable. We went to bed hoping that tomorrow would be different.

Tomorrow dawned hazy. Our well-laid plans for the day just went up in smoke and my humans had some decisions to make. Stay on or go home early? After much debate, my two highly educated companions concluded that we would cut short our stay in Bend by a day and leave the next morning. I had reached that conclusion in ten seconds. Bad visibility, bad air here. Go home to clear visibility, cleaner air...not that hard, even for a fur-brain like me.

AC and I went on a walk the next morning and I almost never made it home.

We were out for Zen's evening walk on the trail near the river. It was very hazy and the rising sun cast an eerie halo. DC was walking a few feet behind me. A few feet ahead, an unleashed Zen was trotting along the trail, sniffing and marking the bushes. He stopped at one bush and froze, staring intently at something behind.

Coyote, I thought, remembering an encounter with one on the Stanford trail. A hare erupted from behind the bush and took off toward the hotel gardens. Zen promptly gave chase. The hare, with Zen hot on its heels, zigzagged through the gardens and into the parking lot.

"Zen, Stop. ZEN! STOP!" I yelled. He ignored me. I ran after them. I had visions of Zen getting run over by a car or a truck. "ZEN NO! STOP!" I yelled again. The cry fell on deaf ears.

Just then, the hare reversed course down a slope and headed back toward some rocks and bushes along the river. Zen followed and, unable to stop in time, tripped over a rock and landed on his back in some bushes. He scrambled to his feet and resumed the chase. Both disappeared into the haze beyond the bushes. I couldn't see him.

"Oh my God! Is he hurt? Zen, come here!"

"ZEN...ZEN!" I called loudly. No response. The silence was frightening.

I heard DC whistling behind me, the short, sharp whistle which always brought Zen back. There was no sign of him. We peered into the thick soupy haze and I could feel panic rising. It was the same feeling that would wake me up when I had nightmares in which I lost Zen. This time it was real. God…. Have I lost him?

Every rational thought was driven from my mind and I could feel the tears welling up. There was a lump in my throat. I can't lose him. I don't want to lose him.

I stumbled over a rock and almost fell down the slope. DC caught me just in time. Again, DC whistled. "Zen, come here, boy." No Zen.

"He will come. Don't worry," said DC.

I turned and snapped, "What do you mean, don't worry? I can't see him. He may have fallen into the river. What if he has broken his leg? STUPID dog. I should never have let YOU unleash him."

Both of us just stood there. Quietly…straining our ears for any sound. Eyes searching the trail in front, hoping that a goofy dog would emerge from the gloom. Nothing!

DC whistled once more—the higher-pitched frequency of a whistle goes further than a shout. "Zen doggy," I added in chorus.

A few feet ahead, a dog emerged from the gloom. It was on a leash and accompanied by a young girl in running gear wearing headphones. I waved at her to stop and asked, "Have you seen a golden-colored Lab back there?"

She took off her headphones. "Sorry, what?"

I repeated, "Did you see a Lab back there? Our dog went off chasing a hare and he has gone missing. We haven't seen him for a few minutes."

"No. I haven't seen him," said the girl.

A sick, nauseous feeling welled up. I want to throw up! I had no idea how much time had passed. It seemed like forever.

Through the fog of my fear, I heard DC say, "Let's walk back to where he went off into the bushes. He might come back there. The last time he went missing like this at Bedwell, he came back to the same spot where he had left me. If we move around, we may not find him."

"When did he go missing at Bedwell? You never told me anything."

"You were traveling. We met Joel walking Chloe. He took off to play with her and disappeared over the hill. I couldn't see him. I went around the trail and even asked a couple of walkers if they had seen him. None of them had. I was hoping that he would follow Chloe to the car. They were parked next to me. So I started walking toward our car. Then he came around a bend as if nothing had happened."

"Is this supposed to make me feel better? You haven't trained that dog properly," I said in an accusatory tone. I wanted to blame DC for this disaster, unleashing Zen, letting him run on the trail. I needed someone to blame. What if we never find him? Poor puppy. My mind was running in overdrive with doomsday scenarios. Which wasn't helping my blood pressure and my nausea.

We got back to the spot where Zen had taken a tumble and there was no sign of him. By now, the tears were flowing freely. "I don't want to lose my puppy. I don't." The sick feeling in my stomach intensified and I was on the verge of throwing up. Another whistle from DC, followed by, "ZEN." Again, nothing!

After what seemed like an eternity, a shadowy figure emerged from the bushes. ZEN! He's alive.

Zen trotted up to us, wagging his tail with a happy smile on his face, completely oblivious to the drama he had caused. My relief gave way to anger.

"BAD DOG!" I yelled when he walked over. "BAD DOG! Why did you have to chase that thing? What if you had broken a leg or gone under the truck? Stupid dog!"

Zen stopped and gave me the look he always does when I am mad at him. It's a "I am sorry" look. Then he began his "Don't be mad at me" routine. Happy hip wiggling dance, body rub along my legs, chuffing in happiness. I thought, How can you be mad at such an adorable creature? *For all the grief he caused me, he was still my pup.*

I heard the whistle and trotted back to where AC was standing. *WOOHOO! That was fun,* I thought as I emerged from the bush and shook some leaves off. Then I heard AC say "BAD DOG!"

Ooh. That's not good. Why was AC yelling at me? I just had fun chasing that rabbit and AC was mad about that? What did I do? Truck…what truck? I never saw one.

AC sounded so unhappy that I thought it best to turn on my appeasement charm button: the laid-back ears, wide, happy grin, and furious wiggles of the hips and tail. I tried once, no response. I tried again, no reaction…. I succeeded after three attempts and AC bent down to pat my head and brush off some leaves. All was good with the world. Oh yeah!

On our way back home, we decided to stop at Klamath Falls. I figured that a name like Klamath Falls in pretty Oregon will be a nice place to visit. So I said to AC, "I heard Klamath Falls is really pretty, so let's visit the falls on our way home." We reached our destination and there was no waterfall. Oh no. This is like AC's futile hunt for the mysterious sculpture, *I thought. As we discovered, there are no waterfalls in Klamath Falls. It's a small town with a pretty Main Street. The town was originally called Linkville. There were a series of rapids in the Link River, which ran through town, flowing from the upper Klamath Lake to the lower lake. The Klamath Indian name for the rapids, Tiwishkeni, meant "rush of falling waters place." In 1893, Linkville was renamed as Klamath Falls. In 1921, a hydro-electric dam built on the site eliminated the "falls." One more episode in the elusive hunt for riches; the forty-niners*

went looking for gold, we went looking for sculptures and waterfalls.

The proverbial icing on the cake of misconceived names was another town called Weed. There was no weed to be found, but I found the meatloaf in a 1950s diner to be exquisitely mouthwatering.

The drive back on that final evening was somber. AC and DC were unnaturally quiet, a pensive air permeating the car.

Was this the end of the road? I thought. An exciting two months were to come to an end. What I did not know at that time was that my future was rosier than I thought. It included a massive 5,000-square-foot house on a 30,000-square-foot property with a giant backyard and a gate that opened on to a trail adjacent to the Dish for me to run around unhindered by a leash. It also included very friendly Stanford faculty members, and their dogs and my buddy Max.

"Welcome back home," said Rod as he opened the door and hugged DC. The tailgate swung up. I looked out and sniffed the air, *Yes. It is good to be back.*

CHAPTER 18

The Beauty of This Giant Land

I was sitting alone, working on my computer in the little alcove that looked into the backyard. The sun was setting over the thick copse of trees bordering the house, the golden rays peeping through the foliage and settling on Zen, who was snoozing on the lawn. It had been almost a week since we finished our trip and moved into this home in Stanford. Looking at Zen, I thought, *He must be such a happy puppy. None of the cramped hotel rooms and strange smells and sounds. No more jumping in and out of the car or settling into the padded enclosure in the back.* His toys were strewn around the lawn, the favorite singing monkey still within paw's reach. In my mind's eye, I could visualize him in the middle of a Zoomie. Such cute, unadulterated pleasure that only he can exhibit. He had been doing them a lot in this house.

I never knew what set him off; it could be a squirrel near the fence or a rabbit in the bushes.

I guessed this nap was his way of saying, "Ah. You can travel thousands of miles, but there is no place like home." The monumental road trip had ended, a truly epic journey that will remain permanently etched in our beings. I felt a sense of achievement in being able to complete such a long road journey. My worst fears did not come true. My marriage was still intact. We had no major breakdowns and only one life-threatening incident. Zen had traveled well. No injuries, no serious illness. The gods had truly been kind to us. Little did I know that he would suffer a life-threatening injury in the future and my faith would be tested.

We had driven more than 15,000 miles across 29 states, staying in 33 different residences—dingy motels, great hotels, fancy resorts, and cozy Airbnbs. We had visited 22 national parks, had enjoyed memorable breakfasts in cute cafes, simple Subway lunches at gas stations, and scenic dinners in exotic locales. The vast brown wheat fields in Montana are as mesmerizing as the green rows of corn in Kansas. We met people from diverse communities, immersed ourselves in the islands of small town culture and ran away from the mega-cities, everything that forms the tapestry that is America. A patchwork of memories welled up: the smile of the woman behind the counter at Mama Hawk's in Hamilton, Missouri; the friendly and welcoming "How are you today?" in a grocery store in Browning, Montana; the very large, bearded and tattooed Harley biker in Mount Rushmore who dog-sat Zen while we shopped. The sight of two road tripping Indians in a car with an Australian dog did not surprise any of them. We always felt welcome. Maybe the dog was responsible for the welcome!

Nothing beats the joy of discovery on a road journey. The anticipation of the unexpected as you turn a corner is thrilling. Will it be pleasant surprise or a rude shock? Does one feel the pain of racism or the warmth of inclusion? We never experienced the former and had several occasions to appreciate the latter, like the friendly old lady at the Pony Express Station Museum in Gothenburg. After sharing a cookie with Zen, she chatted about some important exhibits and by the time we left, I knew all about her family. I wondered, *How would we have ever discovered this if we hadn't spent all those months on the road?*

The vastness of this country opens up your horizons, fires up your imagination, and accords you the privilege to live the "American dream," as millions of immigrants have done over the last 300 years. I learned that Americans can be incredibly generous. Mahatma Gandhi famously said, "The greatness of a nation and its moral progress can be judged by the way its animals are treated." These words rang true on every little interaction that complete strangers had with Zen. In California, dogs are not allowed into establishments that serve food. Despite that, a Subway manager at a gas station invited all of us to sit inside so that we wouldn't be baking in the afternoon heat. I remember her words. "Please come in and sit near the door. Anyway, there's nobody around."

Routine builds comfort and is good for a happy partnership. We had a routine for a "driving" day and another one for the "staying" day. On "driving" day, Zen and I would wake up and go for our morning walk around 6:30 AM. AC would wake up little later around 7 AM. While Zen was wolfing down his morning meal, AC would pack up and then we would load the car. After that, AC would check out and we would head for our Google- or Yelp-recommended breakfast cafe. On "staying" days, the routine was pretty similar except AC would wake up a little later after Zen had finished eating. I would have gone out to pick up a cup of coffee from the lobby or the nearest cafe. I would return around 9 AM and then we would plan the rest of the day.

A revelation of the road trip was AC's ability to keep down her breakfast or lunch. She never liked any road journey because she was very prone to car sickness. Surprisingly, it never surfaced even once. She had built a routine to make sure that it never happened—drive for half an hour after a meal, then hand over the controls to me, plug in her earphones, and listen to audiobooks. She must have finished listening to at least a dozen on all our trips. It also proved to me that she could handle road trips, but only if Zen was with us.

A big sign at Rocky Mountain National Park stayed in my mind:

Advice from a River

Go with the flow,
Immerse yourself in nature,
Slow down and meander,
Go around the obstacles,
Be thoughtful of those downstream,
Stay current,
The beauty is in the journey.

APPENDIX A

B ased on our experience, here are some tips for traveling with a dog:

1. Expedia is a very good site for booking hotels or motels which allow dogs. Make sure the "dog" filter is on and it will display more accurate results.

2. Call the hotel before booking or read the fine print on the Expedia page about the size of dog and the number of dogs allowed. A lot of pet friendly hotels are only friendly to dogs that weigh up to 40 lbs.

3. Check if there is a cleaning fee. Most hotels will take a pet cleaning fee deposit which is refunded on checkout, assuming your pet has had no accidents in the room. Others charge a non-refundable amount.

4. Some of the hotels typically reserve a certain set of room numbers for guests with pets. Check that the room is clean before you walk in with your

dog. Occasionally, the cleaning staff have been a tad careless and though your dog may love the smell, you definitely will not. Make sure the room is clean when you check out. Use odor removing sprays if you detect doggy smells. We had packed one in Zen's daily go-bag.

5. If you have a choice, ask for a room on the ground floor near an exit. It is much easier to take your four-legged travel companion for his daily routine, discreetly, without disturbing the other guests.

6. Hang a "Dog Inside" sign on the door to warn housecleaning staff.

7. Try and make your dog's slumber quarters in the corner of the room farthest from the door. We made the mistake of keeping Zen's bed near the entrance once and were warned noisily about intruders walking along the hallway. Suffice it to say that we hastily rearranged his bedding before other guests complained.

8. Do not leave your dog alone in the room if you can do so. It is a strange new place for him and dogs don't do well with unfamiliar surroundings. It is stressful and they tend to vocalize this stress, potentially giving your fellow guests a rough time. We took this opportunity to visit pet friendly restaurants and there was never a shortage of them, even in the smallest town.

9. Gauge the friendliness of the staff by how the person at reception greets your pooch. In our entire travels, we had only one time where there was a grumpy, unfriendly old lady behind the reception desk. All other times, the staff would have an endearing conversation with Zen, accompanied with treats. As mentioned earlier, America is a dog-loving nation and it was true for all our trips.

10. All rest stops on the expressway have a "pets only area." Suggest you reconnoiter the area before your let your dog out in it. We came across some incredibly filthy ones that had a minefield of dog deposits.

11. We chose not to stay in downtowns; too much concrete.

12. We booked hotels with close proximity to large green areas or parks. Even in New York, a concrete jungle, our hotel was near Central Park. Google Maps Satellite view is your friend.

ABOUT THE AUTHOR

Abhi shares a spiritual connection with dogs and is a certified dog trainer. After a successful corporate career, he went to Stanford and is now a life design coach. He enjoys writing, road trips and has traveled to 45 countries. He and his wife live in Singapore with their pup, Zoom.

He can be contacted at abhi@alt-lyf.com